FAERIE STORM

ADAM J WRIGHT

THE HARBINGER PI SERIES

LOST SOUL

BURIED MEMORY

DARK MAGIC

DEAD GROUND

SHADOW LAND

MIDNIGHT BLOOD

TWILIGHT HEART

FAERIE STORM

This book is dedicated to you

"So do you think you can help me?" the middle-aged man sitting at the other side my desk asked. He was smartly dressed in a suit and tie, which clashed with the fact that his long gray hair was tied back into a ponytail.

While he waited for me to answer, I realized I'd zoned out while he was telling me why he was here in my office. Not a great thing to do in front of a potential client. "Of course I can help, Mr Pelletier," I said, not knowing what I was promising. At least I remembered the guy's name.

Carlton, who was sitting beside Mr Pelletier and taking notes, cut in to save me. "Mr Harbinger will make a start on your case right away, sir. It isn't often that a case of suspected demon possession comes our way and we'll be happy to investigate." When he mentioned demon possession, he shot me a look that told me he knew I'd missed that part of the conversation. He was trying to jog my memory but to no avail.

During the interview, my mind had drifted back to my house where Excalibur sat waiting in the basement. I could hardly get the sword out of my head after Merlin had placed it in my hands to stop me passing out from exhaustion. That had been only yesterday but I was already craving another rush of power from the ancient blade. Maybe it was a good thing I was at the office and unable to get a fix so easily.

"I don't know where else to turn," Mr Pelletier said, looking down at his intertwined hands mournfully. "Since her mother died, Cathy has been my only family. The thought of what's happening to her breaks my heart. If there's anything I can do to get my daughter back— anything at all—I'll do it."

"I'll do everything I can to help," I assured him.

"Thank you, Mr Harbinger," he said, getting up and leaning over the desk to shake my hand.

His grip was stronger than I'd expected, his blue eyes steady as they fixed on mine. "I'm sure I made the right decision coming here."

"You certainly did, sir," Carlton said, touching Pelletier gently on the shoulder and leading him out of the office. "Now if you'd like to walk this way, we can discuss billing." He led our new client out into the hallway and closed my office door behind him, leaving me alone in the room.

I went to the window and looked down at Main Street. There was no rain today, so far, but a chill wind had blown into Dearmont and most of the townsfolk seemed to be staying at home. Only a few brave souls could be seen on the street going about their business.

Hopefully, a new case would take my mind off the damned sword. I wasn't exactly sure when my dependence on the weapon's energy had started —maybe the first time it had called my name from the basement—but it had to stop. Between this new case, the Midnight Cabal, and Merlin acting suspiciously, I had enough on my plate. I couldn't deal with some sort of paranormal addiction as well as everything else that was going on.

I watched as Mr Pelletier—if he'd given his first name, I didn't remember it—left the building and walked along Main Street, pulling up the collar of his coat against the wind.

Carlton knocked on my door.

"Come in," I told him.

He entered with a grin on his face. "I got our new case squared away. Looks like things will be going back to normal around here."

I frowned at him. "Back to normal? What do you mean?"

"Just that we have a regular case with a

3

regular client. No more trips to Egypt or dealing with the Midnight Cabal. This one sounds nice and simple and not too dangerous."

I gestured to the notebook in his hand. "Remind me of the details."

He pursed his lips and looked at me disapprovingly. "Yeah, you kinda spaced out there for a while, didn't you? You didn't hear a word he said."

"Just give me a rundown of what he told us," I said, going back to my chair and dropping into it. I wasn't going to tell Carlton anything about my problems with Excalibur. I still didn't exactly trust the guy.

He consulted his notes. "Dan Pelletier is a software designer who moved from New York City to Greenville a year ago. He has a fourteen-year-old daughter named Cathy. According to Mr Pelletier, after they moved into their new house, Cathy became friends with a girl who lived next door, Lydia Cornell. Lydia was the same age as Cathy and the two girls became fast friends. They rode the school bus together and after they got home, they played in the woods until their parents called them in for supper."

He flipped the page on his notebook before continuing. "Three months ago, the girls went missing. They went into the woods as usual but this time, they didn't answer their phones when their parents called them. The police searched for the girls but didn't find anything. The woods up there are vast and dense so the officers didn't cover much ground before it got dark and they had to call off the search until the next day. The next morning, Cathy showed up. She was covered in cuts and grazes but was otherwise unharmed physically. Mentally, however, she seemed to be "damaged" according to her father. She hasn't spoken to anyone since that night in the woods and she's withdrawn into herself."

"What about Lydia?" I asked.

"She's still missing. Nobody knows what happened to her and Cathy isn't telling. The police resumed their search for Lydia but they didn't find her."

"So why has Pelletier come to a Preternatural Investigator? Where does suspected demon possession come into it?"

"I was getting to that." He flipped the page of his notebook again and said, "The police didn't find the girls that night but they did find a cave somewhere out there in the woods and according to their report, there were strange symbols drawn on the walls. Mr Pelletier questioned one of the officers who saw the symbols and was told they were demonic in nature. So now he believes his daughter has been possessed by some sort of demon."

He closed the notebook. "That's quite a story, eh?"

"Maybe," I said. "Just because the police officer described the symbols as demonic doesn't mean they were. I need to see that cave for myself. I also need to see Cathy Pelletier. I realize she won't speak to me but I should be able to determine if she's actually possessed or if she's suffering a mental breakdown due to some sort of traumatic experience."

Carlton nodded. "I'll arrange your accommodation. How long are you going to spend up there?"

"Get me a hotel room for a couple of days. There's a place called *Lake Shore Lodge* situated a few miles south of Greenville. Get me a room there."

"You've been up that way before?"

"Yeah, I was working on a case with Felicity. There was some trouble at a mental health facility called *Butterfly Heights*."

"Oh," he said, flipping back through the notebook.

"That place had some history," I told him. "It was originally called the *Pinewood Heights Asylum* and the Midnight Cabal were carrying out a secret project in the basement. That ended in 1942 when a patient named Henry Fields murdered nine members of staff and the place was closed down. Fields used his occult knowledge to transport his soul into the Shadow Land and he became Mister Scary."

Carlton nodded as he reread his notes.

"The place reopened in the fifties as *Butterfly Heights*," I said, "We discovered that one of the doctors was carrying out experiments on patients who carried a faerie gene in their blood. He wanted to develop a serum that would change him into a faerie creature so he could be with a siren that was being held captive in the basement."

Carlton found what he was looking for and turned the notebook so I could see his neat handwriting.

"That's the place," he said, pointing at two words he'd written down while taking notes earlier. "That's where Cathy Pelletier is."

I looked at the words on the page and frowned.

Butterfly Heights.

2

Half an hour later, I was at my house packing an overnight bag for the journey north. The last time I'd made this journey, I'd been with Felicity and we'd bounced ideas off each other regarding the case we'd been working on. Now, I was investigating this new case alone. Whereas before, the trip had been made easier by Felicity's presence, this time I wasn't looking forward to the long drive north along State Route 6.

After I'd packed the clothing and essentials I'd need for the next couple of days, I took the bag downstairs and crossed the living room to the front door.

Where I paused.

Should I take Excalibur?

I had no reason to believe I was going to get into any physical conflict while investigating this case—and I had plenty of weapons in the Land

Rover if I needed them—but Excalibur was more than just a blade with which I could fight. It could also provide me with energy.

I opened the door and stepped outside. I didn't want to become reliant on the damn sword; maybe a few days away from it would be a good thing.

The cold, winter wind buffeted me as I opened the Land Rover's tailgate and threw the bag inside. Leaving Excalibur behind may sound great at the moment but what if I experienced a sudden dip in energy like I'd felt yesterday? If not for the sword, I'd have blacked out.

I closed the tailgate and went to the driver's door but hesitated before getting in behind the wheel. If I drove away now and left Excalibur behind, I'd be too far away to just drive back and get it if I needed it.

The chill wind bit into my bones as I stood there contemplating what to do.

Finally, I got in behind the wheel and started the Land Rover. Screw it; I was just going to have to manage without the sword. Being so reliant on the damn thing didn't sit right with me.

I backed out onto the street and drove away from the house without looking back.

It wasn't until I got to State Route 6 and headed north that I realized my entire body was tense. I was gripping the wheel so tightly that my fingers ached and my shoulders felt like tight knots. I put the radio on and forced myself to relax. *Highway to Hell* by *AC/DC* blasted through the speakers and I sang along, putting all thoughts of Excalibur out of my mind. I wasn't going to let an old hunk of steel get the better of me.

It began to rain, the wind whipping water violently against the windshield. I turned on the wipers and squinted against the spray that was coming up off the road.

When I finally got north of Dover-Foxcroft, I let the GPS guide me to Dan Pelletier's house. The first thing I wanted to do was take a look at the cave with the "demonic" symbols on its walls. The GPS led me through town and then farther north toward Greenville.

My destination was a large house set back from the road, nestled among the pine trees. I drove along the driveway that led to the house and parked the Land Rover by the porch.

I got out and sprinted through the rain to the front door, protected from the driving rain by the porch roof. When I knocked on the door, I got the impression that there was no one home. Still, I waited a couple of minutes and knocked a second time anyway. If Dan Pelletier was home, he might be able to direct me to the cave behind the house. If he wasn't, I was going to have to go searching for it myself.

"There's no one home," said a female voice behind me.

I turned to see a dark-haired woman wearing a blue slicker with a hood that obscured most of her face. She was standing on the driveway, behind the Land Rover. In her hand, she held a tennis ball. A large Golden Retriever circled her legs, its eyes fixed on the ball.

She threw the ball into the woods and the dog scampered after it.

"He went to Dearmont," the woman told me. "He ain't back yet."

"Okay, thanks," I said. Wondering if she might know the location of the cave in the woods, I asked, "Do you live around here?"

She gave me a curt nod. "I do."

I detected a wariness in her attitude that was understandable in the circumstances. I was a stranger and we were in a pretty remote location. For all she knew, I might be casing out the place.

"Dan Pelletier came to see me today," I said, hoping to allay any fears she might have. "My name is Alec Harbinger. I'm here at his request."

The dog returned with the ball and dropped it at her feet.

As she bent to retrieve the ball, the woman said, "You're the ghost hunter from Dearmont." She tossed the ball into the trees again and the Retriever chased after it.

"Yes, that's me," I said, not bothering to correct the job title she'd given me.

She shook her head slowly. "I told Dan it was a fool's errand going to see you. You can't bring Cathy back from the God-awful state she's in. Even the doctors up at that asylum don't have a clue what's wrong with her. What do you think you can do that they can't?"

"I don't know," I told her honestly. "Maybe nothing. But if Cathy's condition was caused by the kind of things in which I specialize, I might be able to help her."

"The kind of things in which you specialize," she said. "I suppose by that, you mean ghosts and demons and God knows what else."

"I do," I said.

She stepped closer, anger burning in her dark eyes. "Is that what you think took my little girl? A monster from Hell? Do you think she's down there in the pit being held captive by the Devil?"

"I didn't say that."

She pointed an accusatory finger at me. "You listen to me, ghost hunter. My poor Lydia was taken by a monster but it was a human monster, not some creature from the fiery pit. It's a tragedy that breaks my heart every single day but at least I know her soul is at rest. She's with the good Lord now and I won't listen to you spouting obscenities and blasphemies by suggesting she's anywhere else, much less in Hell. Do you hear me?"

"I wasn't suggesting anything like that," I said.

"Don't you speak to me anymore," she said, turning away and heading toward the road. "Luke, come here," she shouted at the trees. "We're leaving."

The dog reappeared with the ball clamped in its jaws and followed her dutifully, tail wagging.

I watched her go while the rain hissed down. There was no way I was going to ask her about the location of the cave. I'd been in situations before where my mere presence caused offence and I'd discovered that the best thing to do was to keep my mouth shut and get on with the job quietly.

Mrs Cornell was understandably in pain over the disappearance of her daughter and there was no way I was going to add to her pain if I could avoid it.

I had no idea what time Mr Pelletier would return. That meant I could wander into the woods and try to find the cave without any idea where I was going or I could continue toward Greenville and check in at the Lake Shore Lodge.

Going to the Lodge seemed like the best idea. I could return here later when Pelletier was home. Or maybe I could discover the location of the cave by doing some research. Hell, I had a dedicated researcher at the office; I should pass the job onto him.

I fished my phone out of my pocket and called Carlton.

"Alec," he said when he answered the call. "How's it going up there?"

"I've only just arrived," I told him. "I need you to find out exactly where that cave is that Pelletier mentioned. The one with the markings on the wall."

"Sure," he said. "No problem. Is there anything else I can do for you?"

"That's all for now."

"Okay, I'm on it."

I ended the call and got into the Land Rover. If Felicity had still been my assistant, I'd have someone here with whom to explore ideas but with Carlton being bound to the office, there was no chance of that.

I checked my watch and calculated what time it was in England. Early morning. Felicity would either still be sleeping or rising bright and early to get on with her new job. She still hadn't returned my call from the other day when she'd said she was in the middle of something and would call me back when she had more time.

Maybe she was too busy to call or maybe she'd forgotten about us now she was back home in England. I found the latter hard to believe; I was sure Felicity had enjoyed her time here and she'd become friends with everyone she'd met in Dearmont.

Either way, I was going to respect her need for some personal time and space and wait for her to call me. I was eager to know if she was enjoying life as a P.I. but I was just going to have to be patient.

I started the engine and drove back along the driveway to the main road. As I drove north, I passed Mrs Cornell, who was sauntering along the side of the road with her dog. She'd obviously made up her mind regarding her daughter's fate but experience had taught me that nothing was certain, especially where the preternatural world was concerned.

If this case is *preternatural*, I reminded myself. Other than a second hand report of a cave with demonic markings, there was nothing that warranted a P.I. to investigate Cathy Pelletier's mental breakdown. The girl might be suffering from mental trauma that had manifested after she witnessed whatever had happened to Lydia Cornell. The chance that her friend's disappearance was due to supernatural means or a creature of some kind was actually quite slim.

As Mrs Cornell had pointed out, there were plenty of human monsters in the world.

Still, I couldn't be sure the case was totally mundane either. And investigating *anything* was better than sitting around the office thinking about the sword in my basement.

Maybe I'd driven up here because I was running away from my problems, investigating a case that was best left to the local Sheriff's Department just so I could get out of Dearmont for a while.

They say you can't leave your problems behind, that they follow you wherever you go, but in the case of Excalibur, I could definitely leave it behind. It couldn't follow me up here. Until I got home and opened the cupboard in the basement, the sword wasn't going anywhere.

Some time later, I saw the sign for Lake Shore Lodge ahead. I turned onto a narrow, winding road. The wind had died now and a thick gray mist crept over the road. I arrived at a large rustic building that sat next to a mist-covered lake. Parking the Land Rover next to an old wood-paneled station wagon in the parking lot, I grabbed my bag and entered the Lodge.

The foyer was just as I remembered it; high ceilinged with half a dozen armchairs arranged in front of an imposing stone fireplace in which a fire crackled. The room smelled woody and pleasant.

The white-haired man standing behind the long reception desk was the same one who'd been here when Felicity and I had rented a cabin.

He nodded to me as I approached the desk. "You must be Mr Harbinger."

"I am," I said. I wracked my brain trying to remember his name. When it came to me, I said, "Marv?"

He looked surprised. "Oh, you've been here before. Funny, but I don't remember you."

"You don't remember anything, Marv," a large white-haired woman said as she appeared through a doorway behind the desk. She looked me over with an appraising eye and nodded. "I remember you, Mr Harbinger. You were here with your work colleague in the Fall. You're the preternatural investigator."

"That's right," I said. "And I remember you too, Edith."

Marv looked worried all of a sudden. "You're not here because the Lodge is haunted are you?"

Edith shook her head and sighed. "No, he's not here because the Lodge is haunted, Marv. Because the Lodge isn't haunted."

"Well, you never know," he said with a shrug.

I was sure that when I'd last been here, Marv had professed to be an unbeliever of all things paranormal.

"You'll be staying in one of our cabins, Mr Harbinger," Edith said. "It's quiet here at this time of the year and the cabins are much more spacious than the rooms here in the Lodge."

"That's great."

She turned to a computer on the desk and pecked at the keyboard with her fingers. "Your reservation is for two nights. Is that right?"

"It may be longer," I said.

She nodded. "Well, your secretary Mr Carmichael paid for two nights when he called us. If you need to stay longer than that, we can arrange that." She opened a cupboard on the wall and took out a key with a leather fob. The words *Pine Retreat* were embossed on the fob in gold lettering. "One of our nicest cabins," she said with a smile.

"Thanks," I said, taking the key.

"Just follow the sign that says *Cabins* and you'll find it," she told me.

I went back out into the rain, threw my bag back into the Land Rover and slid behind the wheel. The sign that said *Cabins* took me along a narrow road that skirted the misty lake. The first cabin I came to was *Pine Hideaway*, the place where Felicity and I had stayed in the Fall. There was an SUV parked outside and a family inside sitting around the kitchen table.

I drove on. The road followed the curvature of the lake and brought me to a wooden sign that displayed the words *Pine Retreat* in fading white paint. The cabin had two stories with a balcony that overlooked the lake. I parked as close to the porch as I could and took my bag inside.

Pine Retreat had a spacious living room with a stone fireplace that looked like a much smaller cousin of the fireplace in the main lodge. The kitchen was small but had all the facilities I'd need—a coffee machine, microwave, sink, and small pine table—as well as some I wouldn't, like the stove. I didn't plan to do any cooking while I was here; sustenance would be provided by the local fast food joints and anything I could nuke in the microwave.

I took my bag upstairs to the main bedroom—the one with the balcony and a double bed—and looked out over the lake. This was Moosehead Lake if I remembered correctly, a popular destination for fishing, hunting, canoeing, and hiking.

If it turned out that Lydia Cornell had met her fate at the hands of a preternatural creature, I'd do a little hunting myself while I was here.

My phone buzzed. When I took it out of my pocket, Carlton's name was on the screen. "Hey," I said, "Did you find the cave?"

"Not yet. I'm calling about something else. Merlin was here and he seemed mighty pissed."

"Why?"

"He said he was looking for you. I told him you'd gone out of town for awhile."

"You didn't tell him where I was did you?" I felt a sudden sinking feeling in my gut.

"No, I said I didn't know."

My opinion of Carlton suddenly went up. "Thanks."

"I don't think he believed me, though. He left here with a face like thunder."

He paused and then added, "He was carrying something wrapped in a length of cloth."

"Could it have been a sword?"

"Yeah, it was sword length."

Merlin was trying to make sure I didn't turn my back on Excalibur. He'd obviously gotten into my house and retrieved the sword, bringing it to the office so it was closer to me.

"Did I do right?" Carlton asked.

"Yes, you did. I don't want Merlin to know where I am while I'm on this case."

"Understood. I'll keep looking for that cave."

"Thanks, Carlton. Call me if you find anything."

I ended the call and stared through the window at the mist. I was sure that Merlin had no way of finding me. He couldn't track me magically because of my Society tattoos. Only Carlton knew I was here and he wasn't going to impart that information to the wizard.

So why did I feel a looming sense of dread?

Beyond the window, the mist seemed to be getting thicker, creeping insidiously over the cabin like the searching tentacles of a monster.

3

The mist was still thick and impenetrable an hour later as I drove south toward Dan Pelletier's house. Carlton had called me to say he'd found a rocky bluff in the woods and he'd sent the map to my phone. If the cave was anywhere, it was probably going to be there.

Even though the mist reduced visibility to a few feet beyond the edge of the Land Rover's hood, I needed to go in search of the cave right now. I couldn't just sit in the cabin all day alone with my thoughts. My mind kept wandering to the sword and the fact that Merlin was looking for me. I had to forget about that and get on with the case.

Besides, the mist should be thinner in the woods where the trees would break it up. I shouldn't have any trouble finding the cave, especially with a map and GPS to guide me.

I reached Pelletier's driveway and turned off the main road, the Land Rover's tires crunching over gravel as I approached the house, which was hidden in the mist until I was almost on top of it. There was still no sign of another vehicle so I guessed Pelletier still hadn't returned home. After visiting my office, he must have decided to stay in Dearmont for a while or had gone somewhere else before coming home. And now, thanks to the weather conditions, he was probably somewhere south of here stuck in slow-moving traffic.

Not because I was expecting trouble but simply as a precaution, I took an enchanted dagger from the trunk and slipped it into my belt. I looked over my other equipment but there wasn't anything in there that I'd need right now.

I had a couple of faerie stones that I could use as part of an old First Nations spell that would get the trees to show me exactly what had happened to Cathy and Lydia but before I could cast it, I had to know at least the general area where the event had occurred.

The trees that hadn't seen the event themselves wouldn't be able to show me what had happened. I had to ask the right trees.

I knew how crazy that sounded but I'd cast the spell—which my friend Jim Walker had taught me —a couple of times before with good results. It had helped me find out what had happened to

Sammy Martin, a young boy who'd been abducted by a creature called a Shellycoat. The spell had also revealed to me the fate of Deirdre Summers, a woman who'd gone missing in Dearmont.

The spell might help me later but first I needed to discover where the girls had been when they'd come into contact with something or someone on that fateful night.

Covering the magical paraphernalia with an old blanket, I grabbed my backpack and slung it over my shoulders. There was water in there and some emergency rations, as well as a compass and some last-ditch survival gear. I might have a map and GPS on my phone but I wasn't taking any chances.

I slammed the trunk shut and made my way around to the back of the Pelletier residence. A lawn stretched into the mist, bordered by flowerbeds. A small pond, encircled by rocks, sat in the center of the lawn. I walked past it and reached the edge of the woods. Was this where the girls had entered the woods that night or had they started at Lydia's house?

I stepped forward beneath the trees. As I'd expected, there was less mist here; it clung to the ground and obscured the distant view but I could see everything clearly at least thirty feet ahead of where I stood.

Not that there was much to see. The trees

were densely packed together and there weren't any distinguishable landmarks.

The map Carlton had sent me showed a narrow river somewhere around here. Finding it would make my job much easier because I'd be able to follow it to the bluff.

I moved north, carefully making my way over the mist-shrouded ground. I tried to imagine how the woods would have looked at night. It must get pitch black in here. Cathy and Lydia probably brought flashlights with them to avoid getting lost.

But on that one night, they *had* become lost. Cathy hadn't returned until the following morning and Lydia hadn't returned at all. They'd been out here many times before but something had been different that night, something that had changed their lives forever.

My thoughts were starting to sound like a cheesy true crime show.

I'd been wandering around the woods for a while when I finally found the river. It was slow flowing and pretty shallow. I followed it north, knowing from my study of the map that the river would lead me to the bluff. And the bluff was the most likely location of the cave.

Why would Cathy and Lydia wander this far from home? Maybe they hadn't. Dan Pelletier's theory that the girls had been to the cave was just that...a theory. The police hadn't found any evidence that the girls had been there at all. It sounded like the place had simply been mentioned to Pelletier in passing.

Maybe Dan Pelletier thought the markings on the cave wall were responsible for the so-called "possession" of his daughter simply because he had no other theories. The police were clueless and so was he. Dealing with his daughter's mental breakdown might be easier if he believed there was somewhere he could lay the blame.

I'd find out more when I investigated the cave myself.

It took me another thirty minutes to reach the rocky bluff. It rose to a height of maybe sixty feet and had probably been carved out thousands of years ago when the small river I'd been following was wider and deeper. The mist was thicker here. It clung to me like strands of a spider's web.

I scanned the rocks, looking for a cave, but couldn't see anything that resembled an opening. Wondering how far the bluff extended into the misty distance, I consulted the map on my phone. The shallow valley in which I stood seemed to go on for a couple of miles. That was a lot of area to cover while searching for a cave that might be nothing more than a tiny opening in the rock.

There were no trees in the valley. The ground was mainly composed of rocks and scrubby grass. That meant my First Nations spell would be useless here. Some tall pine trees looked down from the top of the bluff but anything they could show me of the valley would be from a birds-eye view and might not be helpful at all. Besides, they were lost in the mist up there.

Don't get ahead of yourself. You don't even know if the cave, or this valley, is an area of interest in this investigation.

I walked along the edge of the river, picking my way over the larger rocks. I'd gone maybe half a mile when I saw a natural fissure in the rock wall ahead. This had to be the cave.

The first thing I did after seeing the cave was slip on the rocks. I lost my footing and hit the ground with a painful impact. I got up and checked myself over before continuing.

After a short scramble over the rocks, I reached the opening. It was wide enough to allow access and looked like it reached deep into the rocks.

Slipping the backpack off my shoulders, I retrieved the flashlight inside and aimed its beam into the fissure. There was definitely a tunnel in there. Slinging the backpack onto my shoulders but keeping the flashlight in hand, I stepped through the opening and into the tunnel.

The air became instantly cooler. I played the flashlight beam over the walls, looking for the symbols that had been reported to Dan Pelletier but saw only bare rock. The air in here smelled rotten, as if an animal had wandered into the tunnel and died. I shone the light over the ground ahead but saw nothing.

The tunnel widened into a small circular cave that was no more than twenty feet in diameter. The first things I noticed were the red symbols painted on the wall. They weren't exactly demonic; they were Enochian, a magical language created by John Dee, a mathematician, astrologer and occult philosopher who worked as advisor to Queen Elizabeth I in 16th Century England, and his partner Edward Kelley, a spiritualist medium.

Dee and Kelley said the language had been revealed to them by angels and it had been used by many occult orders through history.

And here it was written on the walls of a cave in Maine.

The smell was worse in here than it had been in the tunnel. I lowered the light from the symbols and aimed it at the ground.

I'd expected to see the body of a raccoon or maybe something larger like the carcass of a deer but what I actually saw made me take a step back. My heart began to hammer in my chest. I steadied the light to make sure my eyes weren't playing tricks on me.

A human body lay in the center of the cave. Dressed in a long wool coat, black trousers and smart black shoes. The corpse was lying face down but when I saw the long gray hair tied into a ponytail, I was sure I knew who this was.

I stepped closer to the body, avoiding the pool of blood that had spread over the floor of the cave. Gingerly, I reached forward and turned the head slightly so I could see the face.

My suspicions were right. I did know this person.

He'd been in my office this morning.

The dead man was Dan Pelletier.

4

The police arrived two hours later. I was sitting on a rock outside the cave eating a trail mix bar when they appeared out of the mist, making their way toward me. There were four of them, all male. When they reached my position, I realized that only three of them were officers. The other guy looked like he was in his late fifties and wore a long coat over a shirt and tie. Probably the coroner. He looked out of place out here in the wilderness.

He and two of the officers went into the tunnel while the other officer got a notebook out of his pocket and nodded to me.

He was in his late thirties with a short, dark buzz cut and a no-nonsense face that held piercing blue eyes.

"You the guy that called us?" He consulted the book. "Alex Harbinger?"

"Alec," I said.

He sighed impatiently and fished a pencil out of his pocket, with which he made a correction in the notebook. "I'm Officer Davis," he said. "What are you doing out here, Mr Harbinger? It isn't exactly the weather for hiking."

I shrugged. "I don't mind a bit of rain and mist."

"So you were just taking a walk through the woods, miles away from anywhere, and you just happened to come across a dead body?"

There was no point lying to him. A couple of quick checks would tell him I was no ordinary hiker. "I'm a P.I. from Dearmont," I told him. "The man inside the cave is my client, Dan Pelletier."

His face registered shock for a moment and he looked toward the fissure in the rocks. "Dan," he said under his breath.

I guessed that everyone around here knew everyone else. Officer Davis would be acquainted with Dan Pelletier in some capacity.

Turning his attention back to me, he said, "When you say P.I. do you mean private investigator?"

I shook my head. "Preternatural."

He sighed again and wrote something in the book. "So I'm guessing Mr Pelletier hired you because he believes his daughter is possessed, is that right?"

"Yeah, that's right. He wanted me to

investigate what happened to her. He mentioned this cave so I came here to take a look. I didn't expect to find him inside."

He looked at the fissure again and them back at me. "Did you touch or move his body?"

"I moved his head so I could see his face."

"And you're sure it's Dan Pelletier?"

I nodded. "He was at my office this morning."

"In Dearmont?"

"That's right."

He made another note. "So let me get this straight. Dan Pelletier drives to Dearmont this morning to hire you to look into what happened to his daughter. He mentions this cave. You come up here to take a look and find Dan inside, dead. Is that what you're telling me?"

"That's what I'm telling you."

"Are you staying somewhere local, Mr Harbinger?"

"I'm staying at the Lake Shore Lodge."

"I'd like you to stay in the area while we conduct an investigation into what happened here. If I hear that you've so much as set one foot outside of Piscataquis County, I will arrest you, is that understood?"

"It is. Am I free to go now?"

He nodded. "Just remember what I said about staying in the area. I'm going to need your phone number too, in case I need to contact you."

"No problem." I gave him the number, got up

off the rock I was sitting on, and swung my backpack over my shoulder. I made to leave but then stopped. "Do you know how long those symbols have been on the wall of that cave?"

He shook his head in disgust. "There's a dead guy in there, Harbinger, and all you care about is the damned graffiti on the walls? Get out of here before I arrest you just for the hell of it."

It was obvious that I wasn't going to get anything else out of Davis so I made my way over the rocks toward the place where I'd entered the valley.

Before the cave became lost in the mist, I glanced back over my shoulder. Davis was sitting on a rock, smoking. He obviously didn't take a hands-on approach to his job, preferring to leave the work to the coroner and the other two officers.

I looked back again as I reached the trees but the valley was lost to the mist now. Retracing my steps through the woods and referring to the map a couple of times eventually brought me back to the Pelletier residence.

As I emerged from the trees, my phone began to buzz. The screen displayed Sheriff Cantrell's name, which meant that Merlin, who was using Cantrell's body, was calling me. I considered ignoring it but knew he wouldn't stop bugging me until I finally answered.

With a sigh of resignation, I got into the Land

Rover and jabbed at the phone screen. "What do you want?"

"I want to know where you are, Alec. Your secretary told me you've left Dearmont to work on a case but he wouldn't tell me where you are."

"Why is that a problem for you?"

"Because you didn't take Excalibur with you."

"And why should I bring the sword with me? I was given the sword for a specific reason. The case I'm working on isn't connected to the Midnight Cabal."

"That doesn't matter. You and the sword are one. You're bonded. Excalibur should be by your side at all times."

"No thanks, I'll pass."

"Alec, rejecting the sword isn't as easy as you seem to think. As I said, you are both bonded now. You need each other. If you try to turn your back on Excalibur now, you'll hurt her feelings."

"Hurt her feelings? You're talking about a sword like it's a living thing."

There was a silence on the other end of the line. The implications of that silence sent a chill up my spine. Was Excalibur alive in some way?

Moving the conversation away from that question, Merlin finally said, "Just tell me where you are, Alec, and I'll bring the sword to you."

"No," I said. "Look, I don't have time for this right now. I'm on a case. I'll see you when I get back to Dearmont but in the meantime, don't call me again." I ended the call and threw the phone onto the passenger seat.

As soon as it landed, it began buzzing again. I snatched it up and said, "I told you not to call me."

"Alec, are you okay, man?" It wasn't Merlin, it was Leon.

"Sorry, Leon, I was just talking to Merlin."

"That explains everything. Hey, I was just calling to see if you want to grab something to eat. I'm going crazy trying to crack this Cabal code and I need a burger and a shake to regain my sanity."

"Sounds great," I said. "But I'm not in Dearmont at the moment. I'm out of town on a case."

"Oh." He sounded disappointed but then his voice brightened. "Need any help?"

I thought about that for a moment. Why not invite Leon to join me? I'd have someone to talk to and Leon might offer some fresh insight into the case. He'd been a great help in every case we'd worked together in the past and two heads are better then one. "Sure, if you don't mind traveling north."

"You're not in Canada again, are you?"

"No, I'm up near Greenville."

"Cool, I'll pack a few things and I'll be there soon. What kind of case are we working on?"

"I'll give you the details when you get here.

To be honest, I'm not even sure there are paranormal elements at play here. It might be a mundane case. An abduction and a murder. Hell, they might not even be linked for all I know."

"It doesn't sound like you have much to go on."

"I just got here."

"Okay, so tell me exactly where you are and I'll be there soon."

I gave him the address of the Lake Shore Lodge. "Don't give that information to anyone else," I said. "And make sure no one follows you up here."

"And by 'someone' I'm guessing you mean Merlin."

"I do."

"I'll sneak out of town. No one will even know I'm gone."

"Great. See you later." I hung up and sat back in my seat while I considered my next move. Technically, I wasn't even on the case anymore since the guy who'd hired me was dead. I could just forget about it and go home. But I didn't want to do that. It wasn't just because I was running away from my problems in Dearmont— namely Merlin and the damned sword—but because I felt I owed it to Cathy Pelletier to find out what had happened to her father. After all, he'd been in my office this morning and now he was dead, his body lying in a cave full of Enochian writing. That was no coincidence.

I brought up the Photos app on my phone and scrolled through the pictures I'd taken before the police had arrived. I'd captured every inch of script on the walls and had also taken a couple of photos of Dan Pelletier's body in case they'd be useful later.

Putting the phone aside, I started the Land Rover's engine and left the Pelletier house. Once I was on the highway, I headed north to the Lodge. I'd send the photos of the cave walls to Carlton. When we'd first met, he'd told me he was fluent in Enochian. Time to put that to the test.

Then, when Leon arrived, I'd fill him in on the details of Cathy Pelletier's mental state and her father's death.

The rain came down heavily, tapping on the Land Rover's roof in an intricate pattern that was almost like a musical beat. It was finally sweeping away the mist and now I could see the road ahead clearly.

On the radio, *Bob Seger and the Bullet Band* were singing *Sunburst*. While I sang along, my mind played over what I knew so far about the strange goings-on in Greenville. There was an answer to this mystery and one way or another, I was going to find it.

Despite the fact that my client was dead, I was well and truly on the case.

5

It was still raining when Leon arrived. I was
sitting in a plastic chair on the porch, looking out
over the lake, which was now clear of mist.

Leon's vehicle of choice today was a dark red
Dodge Durango. He parked it next to my Land
Rover and got out. He retrieved a hard-shell
suitcase from the back seat before running over
to the porch.

I stood up to greet him and he dropped the
suitcase, pulling me into a hug. "Good to see you,
man."

I hadn't been expecting such a warm greeting
but I hugged him back and said, "Good to see you
too, Leon."

He stepped back and spread his arms. "Do I
look like I'm ready for the wilderness or what?"

He was wearing a blue flannel over a white T-
shirt, along with blue jeans and black boots. In

fact, he was dressed identically to me except my flannel was red.

"Yeah, you look great," I said. "You want a beer?"

He nodded. "That would be great."

"Grab a seat and I'll be out in a minute with the beers," I said, hefting his suitcase. Its heavy weight took me by surprise. "What have you got in here? Rocks?"

"Just a couple of laptops," he said. "Including the one we got from the Cabal boat. I figured I might as well keep working on it when I get a free moment."

I took the case upstairs and placed it on the bed in the second bedroom. Pine Hideaway might not be the spacious mansion Leon was used to living in but it had a certain rustic charm.

Going down to the kitchen, I took a couple of beers out of the fridge and took them out to the porch, where Leon had pulled up a chair next to mine and was sitting on it while he stared out over the lake.

"It's really nice here," he said as I handed him a beer. "Very peaceful."

I looked out over the lake and took a swig of beer. "Yeah, it looks that way on the surface but a few miles south of here, a man was murdered in the woods."

"Murdered?"

"There's no official cause of death yet but it

looked like murder to me. There was a lot of blood. He was lying face down and I didn't turn the body over to check the wounds but it looked like he'd been stabbed."

"Maybe it was suicide," Leon suggested. "You didn't see the knife he used because it was under his body."

I shrugged. "It's a possibility but why would he hire me in the morning and then kill himself later the same day? And why there? In that cave?" I told Leon about the details of the case and showed him the photos of the cave walls on my phone.

"I guess we need to know what this writing is all about," he said, pointing at the red script. "That might be the biggest clue of all."

"I sent the pics to Carlton. He's going to try to translate it."

Leon handed the phone back to me. "You think he'll be able to do that?"

"I hope so. When I first met him, he told me he could speak seven different languages, including Enochian."

Leon grimaced. "Carlton? I'm not so sure. If Felicity had said that, I'd believe it without a shadow of doubt. But Carlton?"

"I know what you mean," I said. "He doesn't exactly inspire confidence. But the Society hired him so he has to be competent at something. Besides, Merlin was looking for me earlier and

Carlton didn't tell him where I am so he deserves some kudos for that."

"Well I just hope he knows what he's doing when he reads these weird symbols," Leon said. "We wouldn't want him to accidentally summon a demon."

I laughed. "Summoning demons isn't as simple as reading a few words out loud."

"I hope not."

We both laughed and fell into an easy silence while we watched fish jumping in the lake.

Leon broke the silence by saying, "Speaking of Felicity, have you heard from her?"

"No," I said. "The last time I spoke to her, she said she was busy with a case."

"That's good," he said. "It probably explains why she didn't answer her phone when I tried to call her this morning."

"She was probably asleep. England is five hours behind us."

He nodded but I could see from his eyes that he was worried about something.

"What's up?"

He shrugged and shifted in his seat as if he was uncomfortable. "It isn't just that she didn't answer; there was no sound at all, as if the line was dead. No voicemail. Nothing."

"Maybe there's a problem with the network or something."

"Yeah, maybe." I could see he wasn't convinced.

I took my phone out of my pocket and called Felicity. If she answered and said she was too busy to talk, at least I'd know she was okay.

I heard a click as if the call was being connected but then there was only silence. I listened to it for about a minute before ending the call.

"See?" Leon said. "Nothing at all."

I made a second call, this time to the Society of Shadows HQ in London. The only real contact I had there was a man named Michael Chester, who'd been my father's secretary before my father disappeared. I wasn't sure I could trust Chester. The last time I'd spoken with him, I'd asked for help tracking down a local Cabal member and he'd sent two Shadow Watch agents who had tried to question me about something called the Melandra Codex.

I had no idea if they'd been ordered to do that by their Shadow Watch commander or by Chester himself.

It was getting hard to trust anyone in the Society these days; there were too many Cabal infiltrators in the ranks.

An operator answered and I asked for Michael Chester. I didn't need to provide my own name; the magical caller ID system would tell the operator exactly who I was.

After a couple of seconds, Chester answered the phone. "Alec, good to hear from you."

"Is it?" I asked.

"Of course. If you're calling about your father, I'm afraid there's still no—"

"I'm not calling about him," I said. "I'm trying to contact Felicity Lake but there seems to be something wrong with her phone."

There was a pause and then he said, "I don't understand. I thought Felicity Lake worked with you."

"Not anymore. She was offered a P.I. job in England."

"Oh, that's the first I've heard of it. I'm not privy to these things, of course."

"Could you give me the number of the office where she works?"

"Yes, of course. Just give me a minute to pull it from the system."

I heard the clacking of his keyboard. Then he said, "Hmm, that's strange."

"I'm being denied access to any information about Felicity's new job. I can't see what office she works at or even what city she's in."

I felt a chill run down my spine. Something was very wrong.

"Hang on, here's something." He went quiet again, assumedly while he was reading something on his screen. Then he finally spoke. "Listen,

Alec, I'm going to have to do a bit of digging and call you back."

"Okay," I said. "But please call me as soon as you know anything."

"I will, I promise."

"Thanks."

"Before you go," he said. "I want you to know that those two Shadow Watch agents weren't acting on my orders. I had no idea they were going to treat you like that. When I read the reports, I couldn't believe it. I'm sorry that happened to you."

"Do you know anything about the codex they mentioned?"

"The Melandra Codex? I only know its name, not what it does. I also know that it went missing from the vaults here. It's disappearance was only discovered recently but the box it was locked inside hadn't been officially opened or checked in the last hundred years so no one knows precisely when it vanished."

"So why the hell did they think I knew something about it?"

"Some magical checks were carried out and the investigators decided the person most likely to have stolen the codex was your father. They came to the conclusion that he took it from the vault years ago."

"But why?"

"I have no idea. All I know is that the

disappearance of the codex has caused a lot of chaos around here. Apparently, it was locked away because it has tremendous destructive power, so the fact that it's out in the world seems to be scaring everyone."

"Okay. Well let me know if you find anything about Felicity. Thanks, Michael." I hung up and recounted the conversation to Leon.

He listened closely and then said, "Sounds like something big is going down. Something that involves Felicity."

I looked out over the lake where the fish were jumping and snatching insects from the air. Wherever Felicity was, I just hoped she was okay.

6

As the portal closed behind the Land Rover, the vehicle shuddered for a second. Felicity pressed her hands against the dashboard to steady herself. Behind the wheel, Thomas Harbinger seemed entirely unfazed by the magical transition from the streets of Manchester to...

Where were they?

Thick woods flanked the road, the shadows beneath the trees impenetrably dark. The road wound through the woods and seemed to terminate at a cluster of buildings in the distance.

The multi-story brick buildings flanked a large green area that was dotted with a few trees and benches. A large fountain sat in the center of the area but Felicity couldn't make out any details from this distance. The buildings and the grassy area made her think of an academic institution. The only thing that countered this idea was the fact that there were no students—or indeed anyone at all—walking along the paths by the buildings or sitting on the grass. The place seemed to be totally deserted.

"Where are we?" she asked Thomas.

"Well, there are a number of ways to answer that question," he said. "If you mean where are we in relation to Manchester, we're in a different realm. If you mean what is the name of the buildings ahead, all will be revealed shortly."

She sighed and looked out of her window at the passing trees. She wished he'd just speak plainly and not try to surround everything with an air of mystery. She'd just agreed to keep everything Thomas told her a secret so why couldn't he just tell her what she'd sworn never to tell? Unlike his son, Thomas Harbinger seemed to have a love of the dramatic. She missed Alec and his plain-speaking manner.

The road skirted the grassy area and Thomas slowed the Land Rover. Felicity wasn't sure if that was because he was being careful on the windy road or because he wanted her to get a good look at the buildings.

"Impressive, isn't it?" he asked, confirming that his lack of speed was to show off the place.

Felicity nodded. She had to admit that the campus—if it *was* a campus—did look impressive. The tall buildings towered over the central grassy area, their many windows peering down like watchful eyes. On the other side of the buildings, there seemed to be a huge rear lawn or fields that cut into the woods.

Thomas increased his speed again and drove onto the graveled forecourt. He brought the Land Rover to a stop outside what appeared to be the main doors of the largest building. The huge double doors were fashioned of a dark wood and intricately carved with scenes of heroes fighting monsters. In one corner, Perseus held aloft the head of Medusa. In another, Saint George fought a writhing serpent.

"Come on," Thomas said, sliding out of the Land Rover. "Let me show you around."

Felicity got out of the car. A pleasant, cool breeze carried the sweet scent of wildflowers from the woods. The water in the fountain splashed and gurgled. She could now see that the huge stone fountain was carved with scenes similar to those on the doors. A diminutive David took aim at a towering Goliath and Perseus held up Medusa's head again, this time against an advancing Kraken. It was from a hole in the top of the carved Kraken's head that the fountain's water plumed into the air before splashing down into the deep bowl below.

"What is this place?" Felicity asked.

Thomas made a grand gesture with his hands toward the huge carved doors and said, "Welcome to Harbinger Academy."

Felicity frowned. "Harbinger Academy? I don't understand."

"You will, my dear. You will. Now, let's go inside. It's time for you to meet the Coven." He ascended a set of stone steps that led up to the doors.

Felicity followed. "The Coven?"

"Yes," he said, touching his hand to the door. It opened, revealing a circular foyer beyond. Wide sets of stairs swept up to the next level. On the first floor, where Felicity and Thomas stood, a number of doors—smaller than the main doors but also carved with scenes of mythical battles—led from the foyer to unknown destinations within the building.

"It probably needs some decorations," Thomas said, eyeing the bare walls. "Maybe some pictures on the walls. I thought we could have a trophy cabinet just over there. But we can get those things later. For now, this is just the bare bones. What do you think?"

"It looks very..." Felicity searched for the right word and came up with, "...grand."

"Grand," Thomas repeated, raising an eyebrow. He paused as if tasting the word in his mouth and then said, "I like it. Now, we need to go up to the third floor where my office is located. From there, I can take you to the Coven. Are you okay taking the stairs or would you rather take the elevator?"

"The stairs will be fine," Felicity said.

"Great. Come on." He ascended the wide stairs that swept up from the foyer and Felicity followed.

"Thomas," she said. "You're going to have to explain to me what this is all about. Why am I here? What is this building used for? What is the Coven?"

"Yes, I do owe you some answers," he said as they reached a long hallway on the second floor. Closed doors lined the hallway and Felicity wondered what lay behind each one.

Thomas continued up the stairs to the third floor. "As for why you are here, that's easy to answer. You are a good person, Felicity. You want to make a difference. That's why you worked for the Society of Shadows, to take part in the fight against supernatural creatures that would harm the human race."

"Isn't that why everyone works for the Society?"

He guffawed. "No, my dear, that is not why everyone works for the Society. Some members have selfish motives and others are there only to bring the organization down from within. The Society has been attacked by external forces and internal machinations for centuries and it is finally losing the battle."

"Is that why you left?" Felicity asked. "Because the Society's ranks are riddled with traitors? You could have contacted your son, you know. Alec has no idea that you're even still alive."

"I can't contact Alec," he said, "If I do, they'll catch me."

"Who? The Society?"

They reached the third floor, which looked identical to the floor below, and Thomas took her along the corridor to the only door she had seen that bore any kind of indicator of the purpose of the room beyond. A plaque on this door read *Thomas Harbinger, Principal*.

"So this *is* a school," she said.

He nodded. "Of sorts." He pressed his hand against the door and it swung open. Thomas stepped through. Felicity followed.

The room had been furnished as an office. A large wooden desk—that bore similar carvings to those on the doors and fountain—sat before a large window that looked out over the campus. A glass-fronted cabinet displayed a number of items that Felicity recognized as magical objects from various cultures. One wall had been fitted with shelves that held numerous tomes and grimoires. A computer sat on the desk and looked oddly out of place among the archaic furnishings.

"What do you think?" Thomas asked, grinning.

"It's all very nice," Felicity said, "But what is its

purpose? It says on the door that you're the Principal but the Principal of what?"

"Harbinger Academy," he said, frowning. "I'm sure I mentioned that."

"Yes, you did, but what does it mean? What is Harbinger Academy?"

He gestured to a leather-upholstered armchair and said, "Take a seat and I'll explain everything. I'm sorry I haven't been very forthcoming but this place is still brand new and I get excited every time I come here."

Felicity sat in the armchair and waited for some answers.

Thomas perched on the edge of the desk. "I'm not sure where to begin. There's so much I have to tell you."

"You could start at the beginning."

"Yes, yes, of course. Well, I suppose it all began in 1682. A group of witches collectively called the Coven banded together to form a society that would battle the supernatural darkness that threatened the human race. They found like-minded individuals and the society grew, eventually becoming known as the Society of Shadows. The Society trained Wardens who lived in each town and city, protecting their territory from whatever evil might arise. The Wardens, of course, eventually became known as P.I.s"

Felicity nodded. Apart from the part about the Society of Shadows being formed by a coven of witches, she knew the history of the organization. "And the Templars, a group of warriors tasked with destroying the Midnight Cabal eventually became the Shadow Watch."

"Yes, of course, you already know all this," Thomas said. "Except for the part about the Coven, I expect. Unless Alec told you."

"Alec knows about the Coven?"

"Yes, he's met the witches. Quite recently, actually. When you both went over to London and your plane was attacked by demons. A very unfortunate occurrence."

Felicity remembered the trip to London well. She'd ended up in hospital after the demon attack. Alec hadn't mentioned anything about meeting a coven of witches but at that time, she'd been having a crisis of faith in herself and had told him she was staying in England and not going back to her job in Dearmont. She'd almost started a new life with Jason.

Would Alec have mentioned the Coven to her if the circumstances had been different?

"I swore him to secrecy," Thomas said, as if reading her thoughts. "He promised not to speak of the Coven."

"He kept that promise," she told him. "This is the first I'm hearing of it."

"Yes, I knew I could trust him. The fact is that due to my obsession with my work, I hardly know my son. But I know him well enough that I'd trust him with my life."

"Wait a minute, you said the witches formed the Society of Shadows in 1682 yet Alec met them recently?"

"Oh yes, they're still alive," he said. "Well, perhaps alive isn't the right word. They exist in a realm where they don't have to worry about things such as getting old or dying." A sad look came into his eyes and Felicity wondered what that was all about but decided not to pursue it at that moment; if she didn't let Thomas get on with the story in his own way, he'd probably get sidetracked and never finish it.

"So the Coven formed the Society and is still running things behind the scenes," she prompted.

"Yes, yes, that's right. The Coven." It seemed that his thoughts had wandered and he was only now realizing it and bringing them back on track. "The witches formed the Society all that time ago. Now, let's fast forward a few hundred years to when Alec was five years old."

That seemed like a strange point of reference but Felicity didn't interrupt him in case his thoughts wandered again.

"The witches summoned me to a meeting," he said. "They wanted me to steal something from the Society vaults; a powerful spell known as the Melandra Codex."

Felicity had heard of the Melandra Codex. Alex had mentioned it to her when he'd had a run-in with two Shadow Watch agents who thought he might know where it was. "But why did they want you to steal from the Society?" she asked. "If they're ultimately in charge of the organization, why couldn't they just get it from the vaults themselves?"

"They can't cross over to our realm," he said. "At least, not usually."

The sadness returned to his eyes and Felicity worried he was going to go off on a tangent.

"So you had to get it for them," she said.

"Yes, I had to get it and I couldn't let anyone else know what I was doing. The Coven was quite clear on that point. What I did had to be in secret. The witches' trust in the Society was crumbling. They knew the organization's days were numbered. They didn't tell me that at the time, they just asked me to get the Melandra Codex."

"So you took it from the vault."

"Yes, it wasn't difficult. As a senior member of the Society, I had access to the vault, of course, so I just walked in there and removed the Codex. It was nothing more than a small scroll so I had no problem concealing it about my person and taking it to the witches in secret."

"And that's why the Society is chasing you?"

He nodded. "It seems that now, all these years later, they've discovered the absence of the Codex and have somehow surmised that I am responsible for its disappearance."

"So that's why you vanished, to get away from the Society."

"That's one of the reasons. The other is that the Coven wanted me to start this academy. So I've stayed on this realm for the most part, out of the Society's reach. I only returned to our realm so I could find you and bring you here. I've been following you since you arrived in England. I'm sorry I have to tell you this but the job they offered you—the P.I. job—was merely an attempt to lure me into their clutches."

Felicity's heart sank. She'd had her suspicions that there was something not quite right about the job offer since she'd first seen the office in Manchester but she couldn't deny that having those suspicions confirmed hurt like hell. She wasn't good enough to be a P.I. after all; the Society had simply used her as a playing piece in a game of cat and mouse.

"Whatever you're thinking right now about not being a real P.I." Thomas said, "Put that thought out of your head immediately. You are more than worthy of the title. If the Society was being run properly, you'd have been made a P.I. ages ago."

"If you knew the whole thing was a lie, why didn't you come and collect me as soon as I arrived in England instead of letting me go through with the charade? You let me pretend to be a P.I. when you knew it wasn't real. You should have stopped it sooner."

"I wanted you to get the chance to work on at least one case. And, as I expected, you solved it. The P.I. title might have been given to you under false pretenses but you did the job splendidly. You solved a murder, Felicity, and you did so in a manner befitting of a top-notch P.I."

She didn't know what to say. Thomas was right; if he'd contacted her sooner, she wouldn't have had the chance to work a case and see it through to its conclusion. He hadn't been letting her make a fool of herself; he'd been letting her work as a P.I. The fact that the Society had bestowed the title upon her to further its own agenda didn't change the fact that she'd done a damn good job.

"The Society knew that you and I were going to meet in England," Thomas said. "I think they used a witch with the power of prophecy to discover that. It's actually clever if you think about it; they had no way of tracking me or finding me as long as I was in this realm so they checked for future events that I'd be a part of. Prophecies aren't ironclad so they helped this one along. Their witch obviously told them I'd be meeting you in England at some point so they got you over to England to increase the possibility of the prophecy coming true."

"And when you turned up, they were waiting for you."

"Yes, but we showed them they aren't as clever as they seem to think they are. There were less of them than I expected, to be honest. That makes me think their operation was carried out by a splinter cell rather than the Society as a whole. Maybe I should be insulted that they didn't send a larger team after me."

"So they want you to tell them where the Melandra Codex is?"

He nodded.

"If they didn't notice it was missing from the vault until years later, why is it so important to them now?"

"Because a new prophecy has arisen, one that says the spell in the Melandra Codex will be cast and the world will be forever changed."

"Changed in what way?"

"All magic will be destroyed. Our realm will be sealed from every other."

Felicity thought about that. A world without magic. Would that be so bad? Weren't all of the Society's enemies magical in some way? Sealing off the other realms, such as Shadow Land and whatever realm Rekhmire was in would protect the human race from the monsters that came from those realms wouldn't it?

"You're wondering if the end of magic might be a good thing," Thomas said. "I wondered that myself when I first heard of the prophecy. An end to the supernatural war between the Cabal and the Society would be a good thing. No more things that go bump in the night to threaten mankind."

"That's exactly what I was thinking," she told him.

"But there's more to the prophecy. The Melandra Codex will be used to save the world from a great evil and magic will disappear from the world. But shortly after that, a magical item will be used to reverse the effects of the Codex and all of the realms will be opened again. Only this time, the barriers will be weak and the other realms will spill into ours."

"So the Society thinks you're going to cast the spell on the Codex and bring about the prophecy?"

He nodded. "It stands to reason, doesn't it? They think I have the Codex therefore it must be me who uses it. That's why they're after me. If magic disappears, the Society will end. It may fight magic but it also relies on it for its very existence. Without supernatural threats, there is no point to a Society of Shadows."

"But the second part of the prophecy says magic will come back. They could just let it play out and everything will go back to how it was before. How it is now."

"No, I'm afraid everything won't go back to

normal at all. The prophesied return of magic brings with it chaos and death. The Shadow Land will spill into the human realm in some places. Imagine what that will mean, what creatures might come through a rift into our world. There will also be rifts between our realm and Faerie. Whenever beings from Faerie have crossed into our world, they have brought danger with them. They are known for stealing humans and trapping them in Faerie. Imagine if such beings could pass into our world freely. That isn't a world the Society wants. It isn't a world any of us wants."

Felicity imagined the scenario Thomas had described. "But it's exactly what the Midnight Cabal wants."

"Yes, the Cabal wants a world ruled by superstition and terror. It wants humans to be afraid to venture out at night for fear of meeting supernatural beings. If the other realms spill into ours, the Cabal gets its wish."

"So you just have to make sure no one uses the Melandra Codex. Then the prophecy won't come true."

He got up and went to the window, staring out at the grassy area below as he spoke. "The spell on the Melandra Codex will be cast to save mankind from annihilation. If the Codex isn't used, every man, woman, and child will die."

Felicity felt suddenly unsteady, as if the chair

she was sitting on had tipped almost imperceptibly in one direction or the other. She could hardly comprehend what Thomas was saying; it sounded too apocalyptic.

"So the Society is right? You *are* going to use it?"

"No, not me. I don't have the Codex anymore. The Coven made sure it was hidden in a place where it can't be found by anyone but can be used when the desperate hour arrives."

The tone of inevitability in his voice was worrying but Felicity had to hold onto a shred of hope. He hadn't brought her here simply to tell her the bad news. The building to which he had brought her must have a purpose. "Is that why you and the Coven have built Harbinger Academy? To change the future?"

He turned from the window and faced her. "We can't change it," he said. "Any of it. The Melandra Codex will be used to save our world and that will set into effect a number of events that will culminate in the biggest threat to mankind's existence since the last Ice Age."

"So what is the academy for if not to prevent that from happening?"

He sighed and let his eyes roam over the interior of the office. "Harbinger Academy exists so that the human race might have a slim chance of survival."

7

The next day, Leon and I headed south from the Lake Shore Lodge in his Durango. The rain had decided to make a reappearance and it drummed against the vehicle as we drove along the wet highway.

I was reconsidering my decision to let Leon drive. We raced along the road, water spraying up on either side of the Durango as if it were a speedboat on a lake.

We'd had a breakfast consisting of eggs, bacon, and toast at the Lodge and now we were heading for Dan Pelletier's house, as that was a good starting point to get us into the woods.

I'd decided that we were going to cast the First Nations spell my friend Jim Walker had taught me. I'd let the trees tell us what had happened yesterday when Dan Pelletier had visited the cave. Since there were no trees in the valley, the spell could only show us the event from a point of view high up on the ridge but that was better than nothing and it was all I had to go on right now. At least we'd know if Pelletier had gone to the cave alone or with someone else.

"This spell you're going to cast," Leon said. "It sounds weird. We're going to talk to the trees?"

"Not exactly. They're going to show us a replay of what happened yesterday when Pelletier was at the cave. We'll be able to see the vision by drinking a potion and using faerie stones."

He glanced over at me with a suspicious look in his eyes. "You've done this before, right?"

"Yes, a few times. It's perfectly safe."

He returned his attention to the road. "I guess this is the only chance we're gonna get to find out what the hell is going on around here. Pelletier is dead, his daughter isn't talking, and her friend has vanished. There aren't exactly an abundance of leads."

"No, there aren't," I admitted. "If this fails, we could try to visit Cathy Pelletier at Butterfly Heights but I doubt they'd let us in through the front door. We're strangers and we don't have a reason to visit Cathy; not one that they'd understand, anyway."

"So let's hope the spell works," he said.

"This is the place." I pointed at Pelletier's driveway as it came into view.

Leon applied the brakes—something he didn't have much experience of—and the Durango slid on the wet highway. Unfazed, Leon turned the wheel so that the back end of the vehicle swung around and we ended up facing the driveway.

"You don't need to grip the dashboard so tightly," Leon said, nodding at my fingers which were clamped on the edge of the dash and turning white.

I released my death-grip and relaxed a little as we drove along the driveway and reached the house. A black BMW was parked out front and I wondered if it was Dan Pelletier's car. Wherever he'd parked when he'd gone into woods yesterday, it hadn't been here; after visiting my office, he never made it home.

Maybe the police had found his car and brought it here, although I would have expected them to take it to their impound lot.

We got out of the Durango and put on our waterproof jackets. I grabbed my backpack—which had the spell's ingredients and materials inside—and we set off into the woods.

The air was damp and cold as we trekked through the trees toward the valley where the cave was located. When we finally reached the entrance to the valley, instead of making our way over the rocks to the opening in the cliff wall, we ascended to the ridge above. It was an exhausting climb; the ground was slippery with wet leaves and the elevation was steep in places.

When we got to the top, Leon slumped against a pine tree while he regained his breath. "I hope that climb was worth it," he said.

I slid the backpack from my shoulders and propped it against a rock. I went to the edge of the ridge and looked down, trying to remember the position of the cave in relation to where I was now standing. From up here, everything looked different. I searched for the rock I'd sat on while waiting for the police to arrive and was fairly sure I spotted it a hundred yards along the valley from where I stood.

"We need to cast the spell a little farther along the ridge," I told Leon.

He let out a long sigh. "That's great. There's nothing I'd like more than more walking."

I picked up the backpack and we proceeded along the ridge until I was sure we were standing almost directly above the cave.

"This should be the place," I said, putting the backpack on the ground and taking two vials of liquid, a scrap of paper, and two faerie stones from its interior.

I passed one of the vials to Leon. "You need to drink that."

He looked at it dubiously. "What's in it?"

"Just some herbs and a little alcohol."

He shrugged, took the stopper from the vial,

and drank the contents. I did the same with mine. The liquid was bitter and unpleasant.

I handed Leon one of the faerie stones. He held it up to his right eye and peered through the hole in its center.

"After I cast the spell," I told him, "You should see a vision of what happened yesterday through that hole."

"Got it," he said. "Okay, let's do this."

I unfolded the paper and recited the words written upon it. I'd customized the spell so the trees would know we were looking for information regarding the events of yesterday, particularly any person or people who had been in the area at that time.

The words of the spell seemed to influence the effect of the potion and I suddenly felt dizzy. The sensation passed after a few seconds and as I recited the final words, a calmness washed over me.

"Wow!" Leon said, "This stuff gives quite a buzz." He lifted the faerie stone to his eye and peered down into the valley. "Damn, it was misty yesterday."

I raised my own stone to my right eye and looked down. Through the hole, the landscape was covered with thick mist. I couldn't see the valley floor at all.

"I don't think we're going to see much from up here," Leon said. "Can we go down there?"

"No, we can only see what the trees up here saw. If we go too far from them, we'll lose the connection. There are no trees in the valley, only rocks."

"You don't have a spell that gets visions from the rocks?"

"Rocks aren't alive, Leon. Everyone knows that."

"Dude, we're talking to the trees. I'm not taking anything for granted." He pointed at the valley below. "Hey, there's something down there."

I followed his gaze with my own but the only thing I could see through the faerie stone was more mist. Then I saw what Leon was pointing at; two shapes were moving through the mist down there.

"Looks like they're walking toward the cave," I said.

He nodded. "So one of them must be Pelletier but who's with him?"

"It could be anyone. There's no way to tell with all that mist."

The two dark figures clambered over the rocks below us. I took the faerie stone away from my eye for a moment and looked down at the valley as it appeared today, with no mist to obscure the ground down there. Then I raised the faerie stone again and looked at the misty version.

"There's no animosity in their movements," Leon said. "Pelletier isn't being coerced in any way. It looks like they're companions, not murderer and victim."

I nodded in agreement. "Pelletier had no idea about what was going to happen."

We watched as the two figures moved to the base of the rocky wall on which we stood and then disappeared inside. I hit the stopwatch function on my watch. I wanted to know how long they spent in the cave before Pelletier's killer re-emerged.

After four minutes, Leon tapped his faerie stone as if trying to get better reception on it. "Do these things have sound? If we could hear a scream or something, we'd know if the deed has been done yet or not."

"They do have sound," I said. "But we're a long way up and the cave walls are probably deadening any noise Pelletier is making."

"Maybe that's a good thing," Leon observed.

The stopwatch reached eight minutes and still no figure appeared in the mist below. The mist in the valley remained undisturbed.

More minutes passed. Leon stamped his feet, as if trying to get the blood flowing in his legs. Standing here in the rain was a cold business. "Whatever they're doing in there, it's taking some time."

He was right. Pelletier and his companion had been in the cave for almost fifteen minutes.

"Could the murderer be painting the symbols on the cave walls?" Leon wondered aloud.

"No, the symbols were already there. The police found them three months ago when they were searching for the missing girls.

He fell into a contemplative silence for a few minutes and then he said, "What if the killer isn't coming out at all?"

"What do you mean?"

"Remember the Pillars of Khonsu? They were covered with symbols and they were a gateway to another world. And there was a cave in the woods that led to Faerie that one time."

I considered what he was saying. "You think the cave could be a gateway?"

He shrugged. "It's possible, isn't it?"

"Yeah, I guess it is."

"Maybe that's why the other girl—Lydia Cornell— is still missing. Maybe she was taken through the gate."

It was a logical theory and it would explain why Dan Pelletier's killer hadn't come back out of the cave. But we couldn't abandon our post here just yet in case the killer was simply in no hurry to leave the murder scene and would emerge later. If we put the faerie stones down now and missed that, we'd be on the wrong track, assuming that the killer had disappeared through a magical gate when in fact, he'd gone home.

"We need to wait it out a little longer," I told Leon. "But if the killer doesn't reappear, we'll investigate the possibility that the cave is a gateway."

We waited for two more hours. Below us, the vision of the misty valley remained silent and motionless. No one came out of the cave.

"I think we're done here," I said to Leon.

"Wait, I think I see someone." He pointed toward the entrance of the valley.

I took my stone away from my eye for a moment to get my bearings and see the area without any mist. I kept my eye trained on the valley entrance and lifted the stone again. The mist reappeared and now I could see a dark figure standing there. As the figure got closer, clambering over the rocks by the edge of the river, I thought I knew who it was. When he lost his footing and fell, I was sure of it.

"That's me," I told Leon.

My past self made his way to the rock wall and slid the backpack off his back. The glow of a flashlight illuminated the mist briefly before the figure disappeared into the cave.

"The killer definitely didn't come back out," I said. "And when I entered the cave, there was no one else in there other than Dan Pelletier. I think your gateway theory might be right."

We made our way back down to the valley and followed the river to the fissure in the rock wall. I expected to find a length of Crime Scene tape stretched across the cave entrance but Officer Davis and his men hadn't bothered sealing off the area.

Leon and I each took a flashlight from the backpack and entered the tunnel that led to the place where I'd found Dan Pelletier's body. The air in here didn't smell a bad as yesterday but an underlying stench of rotten meat was still detectable.

When we reached the main room, the first thing I noticed was a dark stain where Pelletier's body had been lying yesterday.

"So this is the place," Leon said, pointing his flashlight beam at the Enochian symbols on the walls. "Whoever came in here with Pelletier somehow got out without using the main entrance. "I don't see any other tunnels."

"There aren't any," I said. "Your gate theory must be correct." I took a crystal shard out of my pocket and held it up. Its bright glow illuminated the cave around us. "Someone used magic here recently. Maybe we'll know more when Carlton deciphers the symbols."

"Yeah, maybe," Leon said. He trained his light on an area of the wall that was marked with black powder smudges. "The police lifted some prints from over here. Maybe they know who came in here with Pelletier."

"They won't tell us anything," I said. "They don't like outsiders, especially P.I.s"

He nodded and pointed his light at the bloodstain on the ground. "So what's our next move?"

"We should probably take a look inside Pelletier's house. There might be something there that will tell us who he was with yesterday."

"We're going to break in?" Leon asked with barely disguised excitement in his voice.

"Yeah, we're going to break in."

"Awesome, let's go."

We left the cave and followed the river back to the entrance of the valley. I kept trying to fit the murder of Dan Pelletier with what happened to the two girls but a vital piece of the puzzle was missing. Maybe we'd find it in Pelletier's house. Or in his car, assuming the black BMW parked outside the house was his.

When we finally emerged from the woods, we walked across the lawn to the side of the house and stowed the backpack in the Durango.

Leon surveyed the house. "How are we going to get in?"

"We'll check the doors to make sure they're locked, look for open windows."

"And if the place is sealed tight?"

"Then we'll have to break something." I didn't

want to smash my way into the Pelletier residence but Dan wasn't going to complain and if it helped us find out what had happened to him and his daughter, a broken window was a small price to pay.

Leon went over to the BMW and cupped his hands against the window while he peered inside. "If we can hack the GPS, we can find out where Pelletier went after he left your office yesterday."

"Great idea." I joined him at the car and looked inside. "Do you know how to hack the GPS?"

"Hey, you, what are you doing? Get away from my car!" The female voice came from behind us. I turned to see a blonde-haired woman standing at the open front door of the house.

"Sorry," I said. "We thought it belonged to someone else."

She narrowed her eyes. "Who are you?"

"I'm Alec and this is Leon. We're working for Dan Pelletier. I assume you know him since you're standing in his house."

"Of course I know him. He's my brother. I'm Laura Pelletier."

"We're sorry for your loss," Leon said.

She let out a short sigh and now I could see that her eyes were bloodshot, as if she'd been crying. "Thank you. You said you were working for Dan?"

"Yes, he came to my office yesterday."

"Oh, are you the P.I. he was going to hire?"

"Yes, I'm Alec Harbinger."

She nodded. "He said he was going to hire you to investigate what happened to Cathy. It's one of the last things he did before..." Her voice trailed off and she began to cry. The strength seemed to leave her legs and she slid down the doorframe until she was leaning against it while sitting on the floor.

I stepped up onto the porch and crouched next to her. "Is there anything I can do for you?"

"I told him not to get involved with those people but he didn't listen," she said through her sobs. "I told him it wouldn't come to any good."

"Get involved with what people?" I asked.

"They're members of a group with a strange name." She sniffed and said, "The Cabal. They call themselves the Midnight Cabal."

8

The interior of Dan Pelletier's house was plush and comfortably furnished. Laura showed us into the living room and announced that she was going to make coffee. She waved away my offer of help, insisting that keeping busy was the only way she could stop herself from breaking down completely.

While she busied herself in the kitchen, Leon turned to me and said, "So...the Cabal."

"I guess it's not really surprising. In the 1940s, they ran a secret project in the basement of Butterfly Heights—which was called the Pinewood Heights Asylum back then—and that place isn't far from here. So this area was once a hotspot of Cabal activity."

Leon nodded. "And it seems, from what Laura said, that it still might be."

She came into the room carrying a tray loaded

with mugs, spoons, creamer, and sugar, and set it on the large coffee table that sat in front of the fireplace. The sweet wood smoke drifting from the fire vied with the bitter coffee smell for my attention. The coffee won. I added creamer and sugar to one of the mugs and took the drink to a large armchair. Leon and Laura sat on the sofa.

"You seem to have heard of these people...the Cabal," Laura said. "They told Dan they were a large organization but I didn't believe them; I looked up the Midnight Cabal online and could hardly find anything at all about it."

"Miss Pelletier—"

"Laura, please," she said.

"Laura, what did the Midnight Cabal want with your brother?"

She shrugged and took a sip of coffee. "They didn't want anything. That's what was so weird. I thought they were one of those kooky religious groups at first. You know, those cults you hear about. I thought they were after Dan's money. But they never asked him for anything. No money, nothing. On the contrary, they told him they could help Cathy, bring her out of her current mental state."

"He didn't think it strange that they offered to help and asked nothing in return?"

"Yes, of course he did. At first, he was very suspicious but the more he spoke with them, the more convinced he became that they could help him. They got Cathy placed into a facility near here called Butterfly Heights. Apparently, it's very difficult to become a patient there. And because it's so close, it's convenient for Dan to visit his daughter." Her eyes fell and she added, "*Was* convenient, I mean."

I sipped the coffee and let my eyes wander to the fire flickering in the fireplace. Not too long ago, I'd discovered that the Pinewood Heights Asylum had been used by the Cabal up to the 1940s but I hadn't entertained the idea that the place was still a Cabal operation. After Henry Fields had murdered nine members of staff in 1942 as part of some sort of blood rite that allowed him to escape to the Shadow Land and become Mister Scary, the Asylum had closed down.

The building had remained derelict for almost two decades before reopening as Butterfly Heights in 1959. I'd assumed that meant there were new owners but what if the Midnight Cabal had owned it all along and reopened the place to resume their work?

"Laura, did you ever meet these people?"

"Yes, I met them one time. Dan and I were visiting Cathy at Butterfly Heights and two men came into the room. They didn't introduce themselves but Dan later told me they were the two who had visited him here in the house and convinced him that they could help Cathy."

"And did Cathy's condition improve after she became a patient at Butterfly Heights?"

She let out a long sigh. "No, not really. She still won't speak. It's like some part of her mind is locked away. She isn't in a coma or anything like that; she walks around and she eats and all those kinds of things but she won't communicate with anyone. She just stares into the distance most of the time."

"Do you think we'd be able to see her?"

She answered without hesitation. "Yes, of course. That's why you're here, isn't it? To find out what happened to her? That's why Dan hired you."

"Yes, that's why we're here. It's just that we've been asked to investigate a supernatural angle and some people don't like that."

"If you can find out what is wrong with my niece, I don't mind which angle you approach this from," she said. "The police aren't getting anywhere. Besides, Dan decided to hire you because of the symbols the police found in a cave. The same cave where they later found his body." Her face collapsed for a moment but she seemed to force back her emotions. "I'd say there's more going on around here than the local police are equipped to handle."

"We want to help," I told her.

She nodded and gave me a tight-lipped smile. "I'll make an appointment for us to go there tomorrow. If you give me your number, I'll let you know the details."

I took one a business card out of my wallet and gave it to her.

"Thank you," she said. "Now, I have a lot of things to take care of now that Dan is...gone. I'll call you later and let you know when we can go and see Cathy."

"Of course," I said, placing my coffee mug on the table and getting up. "I'll wait for your call."

She led us to the front door. As we stepped out onto the porch, she said, "Mr Harbinger..."

"Please, call me Alec."

"Alec, do you think you can help Cathy?"

"I'll do everything in my power to help her," I said truthfully.

She scrutinized me for a second, her eyes narrowing slightly as they stared into mine. "Yes, I believe you will. Thank you." She retreated into the house and closed the door.

"She's had some shitty luck," Leon said as we hurried through the rain to the Durango. "First her niece and now her brother."

I opened the passenger door and climbed inside the vehicle. "Yeah, the last thing she needs is for anything else to go wrong. What worries me is that Cathy might be in the clutches of the Cabal."

"You think they're still running Butterfly Heights, right? The same thought crossed my mind. But what would the Cabal want with Cathy?"

"I don't know. The Cabal was performing genetic experiments in the basement in the 1940s and when Felicity and I went there a few months ago, it seemed that the patients had been chosen because they had a latent faerie gene in their blood. We thought the modern-day experiments were the work of one doctor but what if he was working for the Cabal all along?"

Leon nodded. "Sounds like they're still running the show. But what do they want with Cathy? Why do they think she has the latent gene?"

"I think the answer to that lies in the events that took place on the night the girls went into the woods and Lydia Cornell disappeared. We need to know exactly what happened."

He started the engine and turned the Durango around so we were headed toward the main road. "That night seems to hold the key that unlocks the case."

"It does," I agreed.

When we reached the main road, Leon asked, "What's the plan now? Are we going back to the Lodge?"

"Yeah, I need to contact Carlton to see if he's translated those Enochian symbols yet. I also need him to look into who actually owns Butterfly Heights."

Leon accelerated out of the driveway and onto the main road. "I'm guessing it's going to be the Cabal but it won't be a company called Midnight Cabal Inc."

"No, they'll be hidden behind some other company name but we should be able to find out if it's the same company that owned the place in the 1940s, when it was definitely a Cabal front."

"You know what I don't like about the Cabal?" he said.

"What?"

"The more rocks you turn over, the more places they seem to be hiding. They're everywhere."

He was right. The Cabal seemed to be hiding in every corner, lurking in every dark place. And something told me it wouldn't be long before it pounced from the shadows.

9

Felicity wasn't sure if Thomas Harbinger's speech about the survival of the human race was a result of his dramatic personality or a sober warning of what was to come. She felt disorientated. It wasn't all that long ago that she'd been in Manchester solving a case as a P.I. Now she was in a huge academic building which Thomas had said was humanity's only hope of survival.

"I'm not exaggerating, Felicity," he said. "The Coven has overseen the creation of the Academy so that humans will stand a chance of getting through the dark times to come." He moved to one of the bookshelves and removed one of the books. Reaching into the space the time had occupied, he pressed a button and an audible *click* sounded in the room. The bookshelf opened on a hinge, revealing a passageway beyond.

"This is how we get to the realm of the

Coven," he said. "I know you have no reason to believe what I'm telling you—I might be a mad old fool after all—so I'll let the witches themselves inform you of the grave importance of the work ahead of us." He pushed the bookshelf further on its hinge until the opening was large enough to let them pass and then he stepped into the secret passageway.

Felicity got up from her chair and followed. Whether Thomas's story was fanciful or not, her curiosity had been piqued. She wanted to meet the witches known collectively as the Coven.

The passageway was lit by a soft green glow that seemed to emanate from the walls and ceiling. Thomas didn't speak until they reached the end of the passageway, where a stone staircase spiraled downward.

"In the Society headquarters building, I had an elevator that descended to the Coven's realm," he said, gazing down the twisting stairs. "It was much easier than this." Taking hold of a braided rope that was fixed to iron rings in the wall, he began to descend.

Felicity followed. The same green glow that had lit the passageway above also emanated from the walls here and the air felt warmer than it had in Thomas's office.

"How far down do these stairs go?" she asked.

"Well, it isn't that simple," he said. "They don't physically go very far at all. At some point, we cross over from the realm we were just in to the witches' realm. I'm not sure where the borderline is exactly but by the time we get to the bottom of the stairs, we've crossed over entirely."

A few minutes later, they reached a small, featureless room made of the same stone as the stairs. A crude archway carved into one wall was hung with a curtain fashioned of strings bedecked with white beads. When Felicity looked closer, she realized that what she'd thought were white beads were actually tiny bleached bones and skulls that looked like they'd come from mice or rats.

"Are you ready?" Thomas asked her. He was breathing hard and Felicity wasn't sure if that was because of the steps they'd just descended or because he was nervous.

She nodded. "Yes, I'm ready."

He brushed aside the bone curtain with one arm and beckoned Felicity to step through. She ducked her head as she passed through the low archway and found herself in a huge roughly circular cavern. The center of the cavern was raised slightly, forming a low rocky platform ringed with stalactites. On the platform, Felicity could see shadowy, hooded figures sitting in a wide circle.

Thomas appeared by her side. "Come on," he said, heading toward the figures in the distance.

As they got closer, Felicity noticed rough-hewn steps leading up to the platform. She and Thomas ascended the steps and now she could see that the nine cowled figures were sitting around a pool of inky black water, seemingly staring into it although she couldn't see their faces because they were lost to the shadows.

"Felicity Lake," Thomas said, as if he were a butler formally announcing the arrival of a guest.

A soft, feminine voice arose, not from any of the figures but from the pool itself. "She has many questions."

A second voice, different from the first but also arising from the pool, said, "We shall answer them."

Felicity cleared her throat and stepped forward slightly. She knew now why Thomas was nervous; a sensation of magical energy swirled about the rocky platform and she had the impression that these nine witches were the most powerful beings she had ever met.

"I want to know if what Thomas Harbinger told me is true," she said. "He told me—"

"He told you of the great calamity," a voice from the pool interrupted her.

Felicity nodded. "Yes, he told me that the barriers between the realms will be gone and Faerie and the Shadow Land will spill into the Earthly realm."

"The realm of humanity," a soft voice said.

"It was our realm once," said another.

"Soon to be the hunting ground of preternatural creatures. Humans will become their prey."

"So it *is* true?" Felicity asked.

"A thread may unwind in a thousand different ways. But humanity's threads all lead to calamity."

"The lost art of magic must be reclaimed."

"A new band of protectors must rise."

"It is humanity's only chance of survival in the new world to come."

So the witches were confirming what Thomas had told her in his office. The preternatural realms would spill over into the Earthly realm at some time in the future and when they did, all hell would break loose.

"How can I help?" she asked. Since the voices of all the witches all emanated from the pool, she addressed her question to the night-black water. As she looked into the pool, she saw faces in the dark depths. They were pale and indistinct— nothing more that fleeting images—but she was certain that these were the faces of the nine witches.

"Help us build the academy."

"Seek out students who will study the forgotten arts."

"Guide them to become the new protectors."

"Recover the magic of mankind."

"Before it is too late."

"I don't understand," Felicity said. "Isn't that what the Society does already?"

"Forget the Society of Shadows."

"The Society of Shadows is dead."

"Infected with a traitorous disease."

"An affliction that cannot be cut from its heart."

"Throughout its history, the Society has fought the few creatures that inhabit the Earthly realm."

"But when all realms are interlaced, the Society shall be overwhelmed."

"The evil ones have been plotting and scheming for a long time."

"And their evil plans will come to fruition."

There was a pause and then one of the voices said, "Will you join us, Felicity Lake, and assist the human race?"

Felicity didn't need time to consider. She'd joined the Society of Shadows because she'd wanted to help people. From what she'd just been told, the only way to do that in the future was to join the Harbinger Academy and recover the magic of mankind so that humans would have a fighting chance against the supernatural creatures that would roam the earth when the realms were connected.

"Yes, I'll join you," she said. "But I have one request; I'd like to warn Alec Harbinger of the danger you've described. He has a right to know what lies ahead and he's my friend."

All nine of the witches' voices rose from the pool, almost in unison.

"No."

"No."

"No."

"No."

"You must not tell him of the prophecy."

"He must not learn of it."

"He has a role to play in the events ahead."

"If he is aware of what we have told you, he might not play his part."

"If that happens, the human race is surely doomed."

Felicity sighed. How could she keep something this monumental from Alec?

"Felicity," one of the witches said. "When you see Alec again, you will have a choice. If you decide to tell him what you know—what we have told you—you will endanger the entire world."

"Alec must play his part unaware of the future," another said. "Otherwise, he will hesitate in his duty and the world will be destroyed by the king of the dead."

"He must perform his duty," a third voice added.

"What duty?" The witches' words were confusing her now. What part could Alec possibly play in the downfall of the world?

"He must cast the spell that has been hidden."

"The Melandra Configuration."

"The spell that ends all spells."

"Go now, Felicity Lake, and remember that when you see Alec, you must not tell him of the prophecy. The fate of the world relies on your secrecy."

"All right," Felicity said, turning away from the circle of witches. How could she argue with that? She knew that she couldn't. But she felt a hollowness in her entire being knowing that she couldn't tell Alec about what was essentially the end of the world as they knew it.

Thomas led her across the cavern, back to the curtain of bone. After they'd passed through the curtain and stood in the green-glowing room at the foot of the stairs, Felicity said, "They mentioned the Melandra Configuration. I assume that's the spell on the Melandra Codex."

Thomas nodded. "Yes, it is."

"So Alec will find out where the Codex has been hidden?"

Thomas gave her a short grin and began to ascend the stairs. "The Melandra Codex is much closer than Alec thinks."

Wishing that someone around here would give her a straight answer to her questions, Felicity followed him back to the academy.

I O

By the time Leon and I got back to the cabin, it was late afternoon. The rain had finally abated and a cold sun had appeared, peeking through the gray clouds like a dead eye until darkness would finally overcome it in a couple of hours.

We were on the porch. Leon had two laptops open in front of him in a plastic table while he worked on breaking into the Cabal's files. I was waiting for Carlton to call me back. He hadn't answered when I'd called the office earlier so I'd left a voicemail. That had been two hours ago.

I called again, this time using his personal number. Again, there was no answer so I left another voicemail. Now there was a message from me on the office phone and on his cell. Where the hell was he and why wasn't he returning my calls?

"Something has been bugging me," Leon said, his eyes still fixed on the glowing laptop screens.

"What's that?"

"If Dan Pelletier put his trust in the Cabal, thinking they could help his daughter, why did he also hire you to find out if she was possessed?"

I shrugged. I'd asked myself the same question a couple of times. "Maybe he thought that the more people looking into Cathy's case, the more chance there was that someone could help her."

"Yeah, that makes sense, I guess." He cocked his head and said, "Do you hear that? Someone is coming this way."

I listened and heard a car approaching. "Maybe it's one of the other guests. There are more cabins along this road."

But when a white Honda Civic came into view, and stopped next to my Land Rover, I realized it was Carlton's car.

He got out and rushed over to the porch. "I came as soon as I got your message, what's so urgent?"

I frowned at him. "I only asked you to call me back."

Now it was his turn to frown. "No, I got a voicemail from you telling me to get up here as soon as I could. I almost broke the speed limit coming here. So what's so important?"

"Carlton, I left you a message—two messages

actually—to call me back. I didn't tell you to come here."

He sighed and produced a phone from his pocket. After jabbing at the screen for a couple of seconds, he held it toward Leon and me and arched his eyebrow in an "I told you so" gesture.

What I heard coming out of the phone was Merlin's—or, more accurately, Sheriff Cantrell's —voice saying, "Carlton, it's Alec. You need to come here right away. Don't call me back, just get your ass over here."

"See?" Carlton said when the message ended.

Leon laughed. "Carlton, if you think that's Alec's voice, you must be crazy."

Carlton looked confused. "What do you mean? Of course it's Alec's voice."

"That's what you hear?" I asked him. "My voice?"

"Of course," he said, looking at us like we were idiots. "It *is* you."

"That's Merlin," I said. "You hear my voice because that's what he wants you to hear. He's obviously cast a spell on the message."

Carlton frowned at his phone. "What? But why?"

The sound of another car approaching reached us from the road.

"Because he followed you here," I said.

The Dearmont Sheriff's Department patrol car stopped next to Carlton's Honda and Merlin got out, looking pleased with himself when he saw me on the porch.

"Alec," he said. "There you are." He went around the back of his car and opened the trunk. When he reappeared, he was holding something long wrapped in cloth. I didn't need to ask him what it was.

"Keep that thing away from me, Merlin," I warned him.

He stopped in his tracks and looked at the bundle in his arms. "Alec, why are you trying to reject the sword? I don't understand. She gives you energy."

"No," I said. "It drains my energy. I was just fine until that damned thing came along."

He offered the cloth-wrapped sword to me. "Perhaps if you just hold her for a moment."

I folded my arms. "Put it back in your car."

He hesitated for a second, and then sighed in resignation before returning to the car.

"Alec, I'm sorry," Carlton said. "I had no idea he'd cast a spell on me. I wouldn't have led him here if I'd known."

"Don't worry about it," I told him. "You were only doing what you thought was right. Now I need to figure out a way to get rid of him. If he finds out what Leon and I discovered about this area, he'll definitely want to stick around."

"Oh?" Carlton looked interested. "What did you discover?"

"I'll tell you later. Did you translate those symbols?"

"Almost done," he said, his voice dropping to a whisper as Merlin joined us on the porch.

"Well," Merlin said, "This is a jolly gathering. What are you doing up here in the wilds, Alec?"

"Just getting away from it all," I said.

He looked from me to Leon to Carlton and then back to me again. "Really?" He didn't sound convinced.

"Why else would I be here?"

"You expect me to believe you're out here taking a break?"

"Yes," I said. "Do you want a beer before you head home?"

He pursed his lips and I could almost hear his brain ticking over as he considered what to do next. I was sure he didn't believe my story about taking a break but I wasn't going to give him anything else. He could take it or leave it. Either way, I just wanted him to go and take the sword with him.

"Okay," he said finally. "I'll leave you to your vacation. But don't forget that still have an obligation to the Lady of the Lake. You're supposed to be looking for the Midnight Cabal."

"Leon's on it," I assured him, pointing to the two open laptops on the table.

He went back to the patrol car but stopped

before opening the door. "Shall I leave Excalibur here?"

"No, take it with you."

"But, Alec, you two are bonded now. You should..."

"Goodbye, Merlin."

He got into the car and started the engine. He didn't look happy but I didn't care. After our journey to the realm where Rekhmire was imprisoned, Merlin had all but forced me to accept energy from Excalibur.

What he described as a symbiotic union between the sword and its wielder was actually a one-sided relationship that Excalibur controlled. Because I was sure that the energy it had fed me was the same energy it had stolen from me earlier when it had sent me into some sort of hypnotic trance in my basement.

Merlin backed the patrol car onto the road and drove away in the direction of the Lodge.

"I'm sorry, Alec," Carlton said. "I had no idea he was tricking me into coming here."

"It's fine," I told him. "There's no way you could have known."

"He's one of the most powerful wizards in history," Leon said. "I think we should all be a little worried about that."

"I am worried," I said. "I have a feeling that he isn't going to leave Sheriff Cantrell's body willingly when it's time for him to go and I'm not sure what we'll be able to do about it."

"I'm sure you'll figure it out when the time comes," Carlton said. He sighed and looked at the darkening sky. "I guess I should get back home. Muriel will be wondering where I am. I dropped everything as soon as I got your—I mean Merlin's —message."

"You're welcome to stay the night and go back to Dearmont in the morning," I said. "There's plenty of room."

He thought about it for a moment and then grinned. "Yes, that would be great. I'll call Muriel and let her know." He jabbed at his phone and wandered away to the edge of the lake as he began talking to his wife.

"Good thing we brought extra burgers," Leon said. He got up from the table and went to the charcoal grill that had been built into a brick pillar near the porch.

While Leon tried to get the grill lit, Carlton returned, a grin on his face. "I let Muriel know I'll be spending the night here. Hey, are we have a cookout? Great!"

"Grab a beer from the kitchen," I said, "And then tell me how far you've gotten with those Enochian symbols."

"Okay, will do." He disappeared into the cabin and reappeared a few seconds later with a beer in his hand. I took a plastic chair from the stack in the corner and gestured for him to sit.

"So, I went through the photos you sent," he began, "and discovered that the symbols refer to a magical rite called The Ritual of Passing into the Eternal Summer."

"Not a very catchy title."

"It's an old spell that seems to open a gate to Faerie. Basically, the spell-caster performs a human sacrifice by carving a magical symbol into the chest of his or her victim and then—"

"Human sacrifice?" I cut in. "There are easier ways to get to Faerie than killing someone."

"Yes, there are but the Ritual of Passing into the Eternal Summer allows the spell-caster to take the life essence of the sacrificed person with them. From what I've been able to find out, the victim's blood and vital organs are magically transferred into a jar. The spell-caster takes the jar to Faerie through a portal and can then use the jar's contents to create a Faerie being."

"What kind of Faerie being?"

Carlton shrugged. "I don't know. An ogre, a troll, probably anything. Faerie beings come in all shapes and sizes, eh?"

I swallowed a mouthful of beer and looked out over the dark lake. Why would someone want to steal Dan Pelletier's life essence to create a Faerie creature? "It doesn't make any sense," I said aloud.

"It does when you consider the fact that the newly-created Faerie being is enslaved to the spell-caster," Carlton said. "Power over others is a strong motivator."

"It certainly motivates most politicians," Leon said from the grill. The pile of charcoal briquettes he'd placed in the grill was glowing orange and crackling, sending its unmistakable smell into the air via a stream of white smoke. "So you're saying this spell creates some kind of Faerie Frankenstein monsters?"

"Yeah, I guess that's what it does," Carlton said. "The blood and guts of the human victim are used to create a new Faerie creature. Pretty gross, eh?"

"You could have told us about this after we ate the burgers," Leon said, eyeing the raw meat patties sitting on a paper plate next to the grill.

"Sorry, but Alec asked. Besides, I wanted to show you guys that I'm not totally useless."

"No one said you were," I assured him.

"No, but you were probably thinking it. I know I didn't do much on our last case but I want to show you what I'm capable of. Felicity Lake is a hard act to follow—I've read her reports and they're so detailed and concise—but I'm here to do my best."

"That's all anyone can ask of you," I told him.

"Yeah, I know but after my last three P.I.s all… died, I feel like I have something to prove."

"Was it your fault they got killed?" Leon asked.

"No, not at all."

"Then you have nothing to worry about," I said.

He shrugged. "Yeah, but you know how word gets around. I'll get a reputation in the Society as being cursed or something. No one will want to work with me. Especially if anything happens to you. Then I'll have four P.I.s on my conscience."

"Don't worry," I said. "I intend to stay alive."

My phone buzzed, the screen showing a number I didn't recognize. I answered it. "Alec Harbinger."

"Hi, Alec." It was Laura Pelletier. "I've made an appointment for us to visit Cathy tomorrow morning at ten. I hope that time is okay with you."

"Of course," I said.

"Great. We can meet in the Butterfly Heights parking lot. Do you know where that is?"

"I do," I told her. "See you there at ten." I ended the call.

"We'll be going to Butterfly Heights tomorrow morning," I said to Leon.

"Great," he said. "Maybe we'll be able to piece together what happened that night she and Lydia went into the woods."

"Hopefully," I said. Discovering the meaning of the symbols on the cave wall didn't explain what happened to Cathy or where Lydia Cornell was. The police didn't find any bodies in the cave when they were searching for the girls so it was unlikely that the Ritual of Passing into the Eternal Summer had been performed there that night.

It was possible that the events of that night had nothing to do with the cave whatsoever. There was no evidence that Cathy and Lydia had been anywhere near the place but I found it difficult to separate the fact that the Cabal were active in the area and the cave was probably a place where its members performed a magical rite to get to Faerie.

Maybe the girls had stumbled into the middle of a performance of the ritual and the result of that had been Cathy's unwillingness to talk and Lydia's disappearance.

If the Cabal had hurt those girls in any way, it was even more reason for me to bring the organization down.

I wouldn't rest until it was completely destroyed.

The next morning, Leon and I drove to Butterfly Heights in the Land Rover. Carlton had left an hour earlier and was now heading back to Dearmont with instructions to find out the name of the company that owned the mental health facility and crosscheck it with the company that had owned it in the 1940s. If the two names matched, then we could safely assume the place was owned by the Midnight Cabal.

What that meant for Cathy Pelletier and the other patients at the facility, I had no idea. Why had Dan Pelletier's Cabal contacts been keen to find his daughter a room there? Was it so they could keep an eye on her and make sure she didn't speak about what she'd witnessed in the woods? Or had they resurrected their old gene project and decided Cathy would be a good candidate for their twisted experiments?

"At least it isn't raining," Leon said, looking out of his window at the dry and bright morning. He turned to face me and added, "Do we have a plan for when we meet Cathy Pelletier?"

"Yeah, I have a crystal shard in my pocket so we'll know if she's under any sort of spell. And there's a vial of holy water in the trunk so we can make sure her father's fear that she's possessed is unfounded."

"Demons and holy water? Sounds old school."

"I don't think Cathy is possessed but I'll try anything to get to the truth. We might as well rule it out."

"And if she isn't under a spell or possessed by a demon?"

"Then there's something else I could try but only as a last resort. In fact, I'm not even sure I'm going to use it at all."

His brows furrowed for a second. "Sounds bad. What is it?"

"A Collar of Truth."

"Isn't that what those Shadow Watch agents used on you when they wanted to find out about the Melandra Codex?"

I nodded. "It is. It's a device that was originally used by the Inquisition in Europe. It forces its wearer to answer simple yes or no questions truthfully. If Cathy is physically able to speak, then the collar would compel her to answer any questions we asked her."

"Compel her?"

"Yeah, using the collar raises some ethical issues."

"You can say that again." He watched the trees flashing past his window.

"It's dangerous too," I said. "If Cathy's silence is some sort of barrier that her mind put in place to protect her psyche, forcing her to speak could do unspeakable mental damage."

"Okay, the collar is out. Anything else in your bag of tricks?"

"Only my gut instinct."

"I'd rather rely on that than a Collar of Truth."

"Me too," I said.

We reached the turn-off for the Butterfly Heights and a narrow road led us through the trees to a circular clearing that served as the facility's parking lot. There were at least a dozen cars here, including Laura Pelletier's black BMW. I parked the Land Rover in one of the few remaining spaces and Leon and I got out.

The driver's door of the BMW opened and Laura appeared. She gave us a slight wave. Even from this distance, I could see she'd been crying. I had no words to comfort her. Only time would gradually heal the feeling of loss that consumed her right now.

I opened the Land Rover's trunk and grabbed my backpack. It held the items I'd been speaking to Leon about, including the Collar of Truth. I'd decided I wasn't going to use it but there was no point taking it out now; Laura might ask what it was and that could spark an uncomfortable conversation.

She came over and said, "I called the police last night to see what they could tell me about the way Dan died. They were cagey at first, trying to avoid telling me any details but I told them I had a right to know and I wasn't going to stop bothering them until they told me everything."

She took a tissue from her purse and dabbed her eyes. "I probably shouldn't have done that; I wasn't prepared for what they told me. They said Dan had been stabbed, that someone had carved some sort of symbol on his chest. That was bad enough but what made it even worse was that parts of him were missing. Officer Davis told me there was hardly any blood left in Dan's body and the amount he lost due to the stabbing doesn't account for anywhere near what he lost. And some of his organs were gone too. His liver. His lungs. His heart. Someone cut out my brother's heart."

She buried her head in her hands and wept.

Leon put an arm around her shoulders but said nothing.

When Laura's weeping finally subsided, she looked at me and said, "Please tell me you'll get whoever did this. Dan didn't deserve to die like that. Someone has to pay."

"I'll get them," I said. It wasn't an idle promise; I intended to use every resource in my arsenal to catch the person or persons responsible for destroying the Pelletier family. The information from the police confirmed that Dan had been a victim of the Ritual of Passing into the Eternal Summer and that meant the Cabal was somehow involved.

Now I needed to find out what kind of operation they were running in this area before I burned it to the ground.

"The best place for me to begin is with Cathy," I told Laura.

She nodded and wiped her eyes. "Yes, of course. We should get up there or we'll be late for our appointment." Her bloodshot eyes swept over the tops of the trees to the hill that rose from the woods in the distance.

Butterfly Heights sat upon the hill; an old, rambling building that looked like something out of a Gothic novel. I could almost feel myriads of eyes staring down at us from behind the arched windowpanes.

We set off through the woods, following a dirt path that ascended the hill. The path terminated at a tall, black iron gate. The lawn beyond the gate was covered with dead leaves, just as it had been the last time I was here with Felicity.

Laura pressed the button on an intercom next to the gate. A crackle came from the speaker, then a female voice that said, "Miss Pelletier, come in." The gate opened with a mechanical *click* and swung open, allowing us to proceed onto a gravel path that crossed the lawn and led to a large wooden door.

Cameras set high on the walls followed our progress as we approached the building.

"This place is creepy," Leon whispered.

I nodded almost imperceptibly so that cameras wouldn't pick up the movement, although I wasn't sure why I was trying to hide the gesture. "Well, considering the fact that this is where the Cabal ran some sort of genetic experiment and is also the birthplace of Mister Scary, I can understand why you'd think that."

"Don't you agree?"

"I agree whole-heartedly."

When we reached the wooden door, it opened with a mechanical click and swung inward. Before following Laura and Leon into the building, I looked back at the high iron gate as it closed behind us.

The lock engaged with a heavy, mechanical *click*.

The reception area looked much as it had the last time I was here; a clean, airy space with a high ceiling and bright white walls. A hatch in one wall revealed an office, which was furnished with a desk and a computer. The furnishings out here in the waiting area consisted of plush vinyl chairs and a low table stacked with magazines.

A dark-haired woman appeared at the hatch and offered Laura a sympathetic smile. "Miss Pelletier, I'm so sorry to hear about your brother. My condolences."

"Thank you," Laura said, taking a pen from the woman and signing her name into a visitor's log book. She passed the pen to Leon and me so we could do the same.

The receptionist passed Laura a keycard and said, "Cathy is in her room at the moment. I believe you know the way."

"Yes," Laura said. "Thank you." She led us to a glass-paneled door and waved the keycard over a pad in the wall. The door opened and we went through to a long corridor lined with doors. This corridor had been here before but now it looked more modern. The doors—which had been wooden before—were now metal and the walls had been treated to a lick of fresh yellow paint.

"So they let you walk around unsupervised?" I asked Laura.

"Not exactly," she said, holding up the keycard. "This will only open the doors we need to get through on the way to Cathy's room. The first time I was here, I got confused and tried to open a door that led to another corridor. They keycard didn't work. I asked about it at the desk and was told that the cards are prepared individually for each visitor. They only open certain doors in the building and won't open any others."

That was a shame. If we needed to do some snooping around, a keycard that opened any door would be useful. Were the bespoke cards simply to prevent people getting lost or were they designed to make sure no one wandered into areas where secret Cabal projects were being undertaken?

Laura led us through two more doors and along another door-lined corridor, only in this area, the doors were numbered. She stopped outside door number 6 and turned to us. "I'll go in first and tell her she has two new visitors. I have no idea if she understands what anyone says to her anymore but I think it's the right thing to do."

"Of course," I said. "We'll wait here."

Laura entered the room and closed the door behind her.

Leon scanned the corridor. "Have you noticed the cameras? They're everywhere."

"Yeah, there seems to be more security than the last time I was here. This place is buttoned up tight."

"So there's no chance of us getting down to the basement and checking it out," he observed.

"Not by any conventional means."

He looked at me and raised an eyebrow. "Do you have an unconventional plan?"

"Not at the moment but we might have to come up with one if we're going to get a look under the hood of this place."

The door opened and Laura waved us in. Cathy's room was spacious and airy, with a large window letting in a copious amount of light. The room contained a single bed as well as a sofa, coffee table, and TV mounted on the wall. An open door led to a bathroom.

Cathy Pelletier was sitting on the sofa, knees drawn up to her chin. She had short dark hair and was wearing a large knitted sweater that seemed to swamp her. Her eyes were locked on the TV, which was showing cartoons.

"Hey, Cathy," I said. "Do you mind if I sit with you?"

I didn't expect an answer and she didn't give one but it seemed right to ask anyway. Her attention remained fixed on the TV.

I sat on sofa and placed my backpack between us. I unzipped it and took out the crystal shard. There was no light coming from it. "Her inability to speak isn't due to any spell," I said. Replacing the shard in the backpack, I took out the vial of holy water. Opening it, I poured a drop onto my finger and gently touched it to the back of Cathy's hand.

There was no reaction. If she'd been possessed by a demon, the water would have burned her.

That meant I had nothing at all to go on.

I replaced the vial in the backpack and closed the zipper. The Collar of Truth was in there but I wasn't going to use it.

I turned to Laura, who was sitting on the end of the bed. "There's no spell at work here and she isn't possessed. I think her condition is psychological in nature, not magical."

"So there's nothing you can do?" she asked. "I have to rely on the doctors here? They're getting nowhere." Her face fell. "She's going to be like this forever, isn't she?"

I didn't have an answer to that question.

"Alec," Leon said. "Maybe you should use the collar."

"Collar?" Laura asked. "What collar?"

"I can't use it," I said. "It might hurt her." I took my phone from my pocket and brought up one of the photos of the cave in the woods. I showed it to Cathy. "Have you ever been to this place? Do you recognize it?"

"The police already tried that," Laura said. "She didn't respond to the photos they showed her. Not to photos of the cave or to photos of her friend Lydia. Part of her memory has been locked away."

"And that's why I can't use the collar," I said. "It would compel her to speak. If she's blocked out the memory of that night in the woods, there's probably a good reason. It's a mental defense. If I knock it down, I don't know what would happen to her mental faculties as a result."

Laura gestured to her niece. "But if you don't knock down the defense, she's going to be like this for the rest of her life."

I opened the backpack. The collar lay at the bottom. Like a lot of magical items, its appearance didn't betray its true nature. It looked like nothing more than a simple circle of iron.

Dare I risk using it on Cathy? If she was repressing memories of something terrible, what right did I have to make those memories come flooding back?

I reached into the backpack and brought out the collar. It felt cold against my palm and heavy in my hand.

In the hands of a skilled interrogator, the collar could be used to extract any piece of information from its wearer. If the right questions were asked, the finest detail could be pinpointed even though the wearer was only compelled to answer every question with a simple yes or no.

It was only because the Shadow Watch agent who had questioned me had been ineffectual that he hadn't extracted the location of the Spear of Destiny from me.

I looked at the collar and then at Cathy. She

didn't look fragile or vulnerable or anything like that but for all I knew, her sanity might be hanging by a slowly unraveling thread.

"I can't do it," I said.

"You have to," Laura said. She reached forward and touched my arm. "Alec, please help her."

I turned toward her and she shrank away from the collar in my hand. She wanted me to use it on her niece but didn't want to touch it herself.

"If Cathy is like this forever," she said, tears appearing in her eyes, "she won't get a chance to live her life the way she's supposed to. She'll spend the rest of her days locked up in a room staring at the TV." She pointed at her niece. "What if that was someone you loved sitting there? Wouldn't you do anything you could to help them? Anything at all? You're her only hope."

She probably had a point. Even though Cathy was in a facility that should be offering her care and trying to treat her condition, she wouldn't be getting any of that if Butterfly Heights was being run by the Cabal as I suspected.

There didn't seem to be any way around it; I was going to have to use the collar. I'd choose my questions warily and try to skirt around the events of the night in the woods instead of blundering in heavy-handedly. No matter how long it took, I was going to tread carefully.

I opened the collar and placed it gently under

Cathy's chin. When I closed it again, the circle of iron seemed to shrink in my hands to fit around her neck snugly.

Although she hadn't reacted when I'd placed the collar around her neck, as soon as it shrank and touched her skin, Cathy threw her head back and opened her mouth wide, gasping for breath like a swimmer emerging from the depths.

Her hands flew to the collar and she clawed at it, trying to tear it away.

Tendrils of smoke rose from within the collar and the smell of singed flesh filled the room.

I grabbed the collar and released it, pulling it away from her as quickly as I could.

Even though the collar was no longer around her neck, Cathy still clawed at the place where it had been. Her eyes were closed and her mouth open as she fought for breath.

I put my hands on her shoulders. "Cathy, it's going to be okay. It's gone now. Everything is going to be all right."

She dropped her head to face me and opened her eyes. Her irises, which had been brown earlier, were now bright violet in color.

"What happened to her eyes?" Leon asked. "Did the collar do that?"

"In a way," I said. "But it isn't the collar's magic she's reacting to, it's the iron. Cathy must have faerie blood."

The atmosphere in the room suddenly

became electrified, as if lightning were about to strike. The hairs on my arms and the back of my neck stood on end. A ripping sound seemed to come from nowhere and everywhere at once and then I realized a bright line had appeared in the air by the bathroom door, like a crack spidering its way from floor to ceiling. The crack opened slightly, becoming oval in shape, and in its center, I could see a green field and a meadow.

Cathy was somehow opening a portal and judging by the scared look on her face, it wasn't something she was doing consciously but seemed to be a reflexive action borne of fear.

"Cathy, it's okay," I said. "No one is going to hurt you. There's no need to be afraid."

Her violet eyes looked into mine and then the bright hue darkened and they returned to their original brown color. The portal closed and then vanished completely and the atmosphere in the room settled.

"What the hell was that?" Leon said.

"I'm not exactly sure," I admitted. I had a couple of ideas about what we'd just witnessed but I wasn't going to expound them right now. One thing was for sure though; the Midnight Cabal wanted Cathy within these walls because she had faerie blood running through her veins. That fact obviously furthered whatever operation they were running here under the guise of a mental health facility.

"Laura," I said, turning to her. "You need to get Cathy out of here as soon as possible. She wasn't brought here because they want to help her; she's here because they want to use her."

She nodded but said nothing. Her eyes were wide with shock and I was sure that the rift that had just appeared in the room was her first experience of the paranormal.

When she finally spoke, she said, "Maybe we should go now and let Cathy rest."

Cathy had returned her attention to the TV and looked as if nothing had happened out of the ordinary. Even the marks on her neck where the iron had burned her skin were fading.

"Okay," I said, putting the collar into the backpack and sealing it. "But I have to stress again that Cathy needs to be—"

"Taken away from here," she cut in. "Yes, I get it." She stood up and went to the door. Leon and I followed. Laura led us back to the Reception area, where she dropped off the keycard, and then we went outside.

When we were standing on the path that led across the lawn to the gate, she stopped and said, "You go ahead. I'll see if I can speak to the doctors about having Cathy discharged."

Before I had a chance to reply, she waved at the camera over the door and it clicked open. Laura disappeared inside.

The big iron gate swung open.

"Guess that's our cue to leave," Leon said.

I nodded. "Let's get back to the car. These cameras give me the creeps."

As we walked along the path, he said, "You think there are Cabal eyes watching us through the lenses?"

"Yeah, I'm pretty sure of it."

We passed through the gate and it closed behind us with a mechanical *click*.

"I guess we should wait until we're far away from this place before we discuss what just happened," Leon said as we followed the path through the woods. "They probably have listening devices in the damn trees."

I nodded but said nothing. He was probably right.

When we were finally back in the Land Rover, I started the engine and said to Leon, "I think Cathy Pelletier is what's known as a Walker of Worlds. The Walkers are an extremely rare race of faerie creatures that can open interdimensional rifts at will. In Cathy's case, it looks like the talent comes from a latent faerie gene. It's probably been dormant all her life but emerged that night in the woods."

Leon nodded thoughtfully. "That makes sense. The question is what brought it out of its dormancy? It emerged in the room just now when she was in pain and scared. So what happened to her that night?"

"There's another, more pressing question," I told him as we drove away from the parking lot. "Since we're guessing that Cathy opened a rift that night and we know that only she returned from the woods, does that mean Lydia Cornell went through the rift?"

"It sounds logical," he said.

"Yeah, and that's what worries me. Because if Lydia went through an interdimensional rift that night, she could be stuck on the other side."

We were on the highway when my phone rang. I checked the screen, saw Carlton's name, and pulled over to answer it. I put the call on speaker. "Carlton, what's up? You're on speaker with me and Leon."

"I got the information you wanted about Butterfly Heights," he said. "It's owned by a company called Paraworld Medical."

"Did the same company own it when it was a Cabal front in the 1940s?"

"Yeah, it looks like the same company has owned the building since it was built. I guess we should have realized who owned it from what Dan Pelletier said in the office, eh?"

I had no idea what he was talking about. "What do you mean?"

"When he came to the office the other day. Oh, that's right, you weren't listening were you?"

"What did he say, Carlton?"

"Just let me consult my notes. Ah, here it is. He said two guys from a company called Paraworld Medical approached him and offered to help Cathy. They got her a place at Butterfly Heights."

"That's what he said? Two guys from Paraworld Medical?"

"That's exactly what he said. My notes are quite detailed."

Why had Laura said the two men who approached Dan were from the Midnight Cabal? Leon looked at me and frowned and I knew he was thinking the same thing.

"What else did he say about those two guys?" I asked Carlton.

There was a pause while he assumedly consulted his notes. "He said he didn't trust them and neither did his sister Laura. So he told them no. But some time later, Laura changed her mind and convinced him that the best thing to do for Cathy would be to send her to Butterfly Heights. They argued about it but she eventually convinced him."

Leon and I exchanged an incredulous look. Dan's story again differed wildly from Laura's. She'd told us that she'd told him not to get involved with the men from the Cabal.

"And then he said that after a while, Cathy's treatment at Butterfly Heights didn't seem to be working so he hired you. That was his sister's idea too, apparently."

None of this was making any sense. Laura had told us that Dan had mentioned to her that he was going to hire me. She never said it had been her idea.

"Carlton, I'm going to need you to send over your notes in an email."

"Sure, I can do that."

"Great. Keep looking into Paraworld Medical and let me know if you find anything interesting."

"Will do. Oh, there's one more thing. Amy Cantrell was here a while ago looking for her dad. I mean Merlin. The sheriff. Well, not the sheriff. The wizard."

"Yeah, I know who you mean."

"She said he's been missing since yesterday. It sounds like he didn't come back to Dearmont after he followed me up north."

"Great," I said. "That's all I need."

"Just letting you know."

"Thanks, Carlton. Speak to you later." I ended the call and got back on the highway.

"There's something fishy going on," Leon said.

"Agreed. Laura Pelletier's story is the opposite of her brother's. If the two guys who spoke to Dan told him they were from Paraworld Medical, why did Laura mention the Midnight Cabal?"

Leon didn't answer for a moment and then he

said, "Because she wanted to make sure you stayed on the case."

"What do you mean?"

"I'm not exactly sure what game she's playing but for some reason, she wanted to make sure you didn't abandon the case. After Dan's death, what reason did you have to stick around? None. By mentioning the Midnight Cabal, she made sure you'd go to Butterfly Heights. And according to what her brother said in your office, it was her idea to hire you in the first place."

"Okay," I said, mulling it over. "But why the subterfuge?"

"I don't know."

"And if the two guys who got Cathy into the Heights told Dan they were from Paraworld Medical, why did Laura mention the Cabal? How has she even heard of the Cabal?"

"I guess the obvious answer is that she might be a member," Leon offered.

I thought about that. If Laura was a member of the Cabal, then why did Dan say she didn't trust the two Cabal members at first? Why had she objected to Laura going to Butterfly Heights and only changed her mind later? If she'd been a member, she'd have tried to convince him to send Cathy to the Heights straight away.

"We need to get to the bottom of this," I said.

"Do you have a plan?"

"Yeah, we can take a look inside Dan's house

like we were going to do yesterday before we met Laura. She's still at Butterfly Heights so there's no one home right now. We'll use the Janus statue to get in and out. She'll never know we were there."

"Sounds good to me."

When we arrived at Dan's house, I backed onto the driveway so the Land Rover was pointing at the highway in case we needed to make a fast getaway. The Janus statue was wrapped in a piece of fabric in the trunk, which I removed to reveal the likeness of the two-faced god. This item would get us through any door that happened to be in our way.

"We need to be quick," I said to Leon. "We don't know how long Laura will stay at Butterfly Heights."

He nodded his understanding and followed my onto the porch. I held the statue near the front door and the lock opened with a satisfying *click*. Pushing my way inside, I tried to determine the best places to search for anything that might help us in our search for the truth.

"You look down here and I'll search upstairs," I said to Leon. I went up to the next floor, where I found four bedrooms and a bathroom. A quick search of the closets in the largest bedroom revealed nothing other than Dan's clothing and some sports equipment that consisted of tennis rackets, ice skates, and a hockey stick.

In a second bedroom, I found clothing and

jewelry that I assumed belonged to Laura. A large suitcase on the floor was only half-unpacked and I wondered when Laura had arrived at Dan's house and where she lived. Dan had said that he and his daughter moved here a year ago from New York state. Maybe that was where Laura was from.

I left the bedroom and called Carlton.

"Hi Alec," he said when he answered. "How's it going?"

"We're making progress," I said. "Listen, I need you to look up Laura Pelletier. Find out where she lives, where she works, that kind of thing."

"Sure. Am I looking for anything specific?"

"Not at the moment. I just want to know who she is."

"Got it. By the way, I've been looking into Paraworld Medical. It's a pretty big pharmaceutical company that supplies drugs to hospitals all over the country. It has branches in Europe and Asia too."

That gave me pause. Could an organization like the Midnight Cabal actually be operating a global pharmaceutical company? That was a scary thought.

"Thanks, Carlton," I said. "Keep digging and see what else you uncover." I ended the call.

I came to the final door on this level of the house and opened it to reveal a girl's bedroom. The walls were hung with band posters and there was a desk and computer in one corner. Open textbooks sat on the desk, along with an assortment of pens and notebooks. This was obviously where Cathy Pelletier used to do her homework before she experienced the event that would change her life forever.

Could there be something in this room that explained what had happened to Cathy and her friend? The desk didn't have any drawers but a small nightstand next to the bed did. I checked them and found what looked like a diary hidden under some notebooks. Unlike its companions, this book had a hard cover and Cathy had applied stickers of flowers on it. She'd arranged them so that they spelled out her name.

I flipped through the book and saw page after page of pencil drawings. One drawing in particular caught my eye and I stopped on that page. Cathy had drawn the cave, as seen from the river. On the sketch, it was nothing more than a line in the rocks, an uneven fissure, but it was unmistakably the cave I'd visited and the place where Dan Pelletier had been murdered.

Placing the book on the bed, I checked the others in the drawer. They all contained pieces of art—some pencil, some watercolor paintings— that seemed to depict the local area. These notebooks weren't exactly handwritten diaries but they could reveal something useful. I placed them on the bed with the hardback one and closed the drawer. Picking up the sketchbooks, I went back downstairs.

Leon was coming out of a side room. When he saw me, he held up a thumb drive. "Dan's office is in there. His computer wasn't password protected in any serious way."

"Anything useful?"

He shrugged. "I didn't look at any of it yet. I just downloaded his diary, emails, and web history so I can peruse it later at my leisure."

"Great. Let's get out of here."

We went outside and I used the Janus statue to lock the front door. I'd been careful to replace everything I'd moved in the upstairs rooms and I was sure Leon had done the same downstairs.

We threw everything into the Land Rover and hightailed it out of there.

As we drove north on the highway, Leon flicked through the sketchbooks I'd taken from Cathy's nightstand. "What are these?" he asked.

"Cathy drew them."

"Oh yeah, she signed and dated them." He pointed at a scribbled signature and handwritten date in the bottom right corner of a sketch of some pine trees. "Hell, she's a good artist."

"She is," I said. "There might be something in there that helps us understand Cathy better."

He looked at a few more drawings before asking, "When did the girls go missing?"

"Three months ago."

He leafed through the drawings and said, "Then there's definitely something in here that will help us."

"Why do you say that?"

He looked at me and said, "Some of these drawings were made after that night."

We got back to the cabin and took everything inside. Leon sat at the pine dining table inserted the thumb drive into his laptop while I took the sketchbooks to the sofa and sorted them into chronological order.

They dated back to when Cathy and her father lived in New York state and the pictures from that time were drawings of Cathy's school, portraits of her friends, and landscapes showing farms and fields.

She was a good artist and each picture contained a spark of life that shone through her subjects.

But the older pieces of art probably weren't going to tell me anything. I picked up the most recent book, which wasn't the hard backed book with the flower stickers on it but a plain looking, spiral bound notebook that was smaller than the others.

As Leon had pointed out, the drawings in this book were dated after the event in the woods. So even though Cathy hadn't been speaking to anyone, she'd continued to draw and paint, probably when she was alone in her room.

The first picture in the book was a pencil sketch of the cave in the woods but it was different to the drawing in the hardback book. I opened the sticker-covered book and found the picture I'd first seen in Cathy's bedroom. It showed the cave as a fissure in the rocks and the scene seemed peaceful. The date on that picture was a year ago so I assumed Cathy had drawn it shortly after moving here.

In stark contrast, the more recent picture showed the cave as a wide mouth that seemed to be open as if ready to bite someone. A black smoke issued from the cave, which Cathy had drawn with heavy scribbles of graphite.

I turned to the next page. The heavy scribbles of smoke were there too, only now there were two glowing eyes in the darkness and clawed hands reaching out of the smoke.

Was this something Cathy had actually seen or was the smoke-creature symbolic, representing the evil actions that took place in the cave? And how much did Cathy know of those actions? Had she and Lydia been in the wrong place at the wrong time and seen something that got them into trouble?

The next page showed a number of silhouetted figures running from the cave and in this picture; Cathy had drawn herself and a girl I assumed to be Lydia Cornell fleeing into the woods.

So it seemed the girls had stumbled across some sort of Cabal ritual that was taking place in the woods that night and they'd been chased through the trees. If only Cathy had shown these drawings to her father, he'd have known what had happened and maybe the police could have conducted their investigation with some leads instead of blundering around in the dark.

Maybe Cathy thought the information in these drawings too dangerous to share. She might have been trying to protect her father by keeping the sketchbook hidden.

So why draw these pictures at all?

It seemed that even though she couldn't talk about her experience, Cathy needed to express herself somehow and she'd done so via her art.

The next page in the book showed a rift appearing between the trees and the two girls running into it to escape their pursuers. I had no idea if this was the first time Cathy had opened a rift between worlds but judging by what had happened in her room at Butterfly Heights, the ability seemed to be triggered by fear, a reflexive action.

Most people have a fight or flight response when they're in a dangerous situation; Cathy's flight response included a portal through which to flee.

I turned the page and found a drawing very different from the others. This was a landscape that showed rolling pastures and distant trees. A castle sat on a high hill and looked like it had come straight out of a fairy tale, with high turrets and crenellated walls.

If this was what the girls found on the other side of the rift, I was pretty certain they'd ended up in Faerie. That made sense because if Cathy had a latent faerie gene, a portal to Faerie would be the obvious way in which her talent would manifest itself.

The next piece of art was a watercolor painting that consisted of vibrant purple clouds hanging over the castle. Dark figures were running down the hill toward the girls. The figures looked identical to the ones issuing from the cave. Had Cathy and Lydia escaped the Cabal on this realm only to run into more members of the organization in the Faerie realm?

It was possible. Gloria, the Lady of the Forest, had told me some time ago that the Cabal was taking over parts of Faerie to wage war on the

Society from that realm. The castle could be one of their strongholds.

The next picture seemed to confirm that theory. It showed Cathy running toward the trees while the dark figures had seized Lydia and were taking her to the castle.

I turned the page to see another rift forming and Cathy stepping through it.

After that, the sketches were of the police officers combing the woods behind the house, looking for Lydia.

The final drawing showed Lydia sitting on the floor of a prison cell, her face turned toward a barred window as she stared longingly at the sky.

"Lydia Cornell is trapped in Faerie," I told Leon.

He arched his eyebrows. "Really?"

"Yeah, look at these drawings Cathy made." I took the sketchbook over to the table and placed it in front of him.

He leafed through it, nodding slowly. "Yeah, looks that way."

"Anything interesting on Dan's computer?"

"It mostly confirms what Carlton told us," he said. "From what I can piece together from Dan's emails, Laura went to stay with him and Cathy a couple of days after the incident. Dan was approached by two men who said they worked for Paraworld Medical, not the Midnight Cabal. He was ready to take them up on their offer but

Laura advised him not to, saying she didn't trust them."

"But she later convinced him to take the offer," I mused.

"Yeah, and something weird happened in between. She went back home for what was supposed to be a couple of days but Dan didn't see or hear from her for over a month. No phone calls, no emails, nothing. Then she turned up out of the blue and was all for sending Cathy to Butterfly Heights."

"So something happened to change her mind. Where the hell did she go for a month?"

"A Midnight Cabal training camp?" Leon offered.

"She certainly seems to be working with them now. I think you're right; she wanted me to stay on the case and bring Cathy out of her non-communicative state. If the Cabal is running its genetic engineering project in Butterfly Heights and they want faerie genes, what better patient than someone with rare faerie blood?"

"But they don't need her to be communicative to harvest her genes," he said.

"No, they don't. So they want something else from her."

"If she can open rifts with her mind, they probably want her to do that for them."

"Maybe, but there are many ways to move

between realms. The Cabal doesn't need a Walker of Worlds for that."

Leon shrugged. "Then I have no idea."

My phone buzzed. It was Carlton. I put him on speaker.

"I did some research on Laura Pelletier," he said. "I got a hit in the Society's database. Do you know a P.I. in New York named Christina Flores?"

"No," I said.

"She investigated Laura a couple months ago. Someone in Laura's apartment building went Miss Flores's office because he thought his neighbor—Laura—might be a werewolf. According to him, she was sneaking out in the middle of the night, especially around the time of the full moon. The case file Miss Flores submitted into the database says that Laura was definitely not a werewolf but there was something odd about her. According to everyone who knew Laura, her entire personality had changed. She used to be friendly and generous but now she was solitary and mean. Miss Flores deemed the cause of the personality shift to be of a mundane and not preternatural origin so she closed the case."

"Not much to go on," Leon said.

"Still," I said, "We need to talk with Christina Flores. Case files sometimes only tell half the actual story of a case."

"I'll reach out to her," Carlton said. "Maybe she can provide some extra information."

"Good work, Carlton. Let me know what she says."

"I will." He ended the call.

Leon got up from the table and said, "I'm going to make us some coffee. I have a feeling we're going to need it." He went into the kitchen and started to fill the machine.

I pondered the fact that Laura had been investigated by a P.I. during the month she'd gone off-grid as far as her brother was concerned. Why would she vanish from his life like that and then show up later as if nothing had happened? The Cabal must have gotten to her in some way but how?

My phone buzzed again. The number on the screen was one that I didn't recognize. I only hoped this call, whatever it was, wouldn't add to the growing list of questions in my head.

"Alec Harbinger."

A woman's voice said, "Mr Harbinger, this is Christina Flores. Your colleague called me and told me you wanted some information regarding a case I worked recently."

"That's right. Thanks for calling. The case involved Laura Pelletier. I understand you were investigating her because one of her neighbors thought she might be a werewolf."

"A number of her neighbors were concerned

with Miss Pelletier's changing behavior," she said. "She became partial to nocturnal wanderings. She was no werewolf, though. I saw her walking the streets—in human form—during a full moon."

"It says on the case file that you determined her change of behavior to be due to mundane means. Do you think she had a mental breakdown of some sort?"

"Hey, there's nothing wrong with deciding you like to take a walk at night," she said. "I'm not sure she had any kind of mental problems at all. I might have investigated further if not for the fact that the case came to an abrupt end."

Nothing like that had been mentioned in the case file. "It says in the file that you closed the case because she wasn't a werewolf."

She sighed. "Is that what it says? My damned assistant is going to get a telling off if that's what he put into the file. That makes it sound like I didn't do my due diligence. After discounting the werewolf theory, I would have looked into other avenues of investigation except suddenly there was no reason to anymore."

"What do you mean by that?"

She paused and then said, "Can I ask why you want this information?"

I probably owed her an explanation, if only to ensure her that I wasn't questioning her work. "Laura Pelletier is part of a case I'm working on."

"Oh? More complaints about her behavior?"

"No, nothing like that. I'm helping her find out what happened to a family member."

"You're helping her?" She sounded confused.

"Yes. I can't really go into details over the phone but basically I'm just trying to making sure I have a clear picture of what's happening regarding my case."

There was a pause on the other end of the line that went on for so long, I asked, "Miss Flores, are you still there?"

"It's Christina," she said. "Sorry, I'm just a little confused. Laura Pelletier hired you to work a case?"

"Well, she didn't exactly hire me herself, her brother did."

"But you've spoken to her? Laura, I mean?"

"Yes."

Another pause and then, "When was the last time you spoke to her?"

"This morning."

She sighed again. "Then I closed my case too early."

"I don't understand," I told her truthfully.

"Mr Harbinger—"

"Alec, please."

"Alec, the reason I stopped investigating Laura wasn't because I discovered she was free of lycanthropy. I closed the case because Laura Pelletier is dead."

14

"Dead?" I felt my grip tighten on the phone.

"Yeah, dead," Christina said. "I drove over to her apartment one morning to find a couple of patrol cars outside the building. The cops were questioning the residents about Laura. They'd found her body in an abandoned building a couple of miles away."

This wasn't making much sense. "And they were sure it was Laura?"

"Yeah, there's no doubt about it. Her remains were identified by her best friend. I spoke to the friend later—despite what the case file says, I investigated the case thoroughly—and she told me there was absolutely no doubt that it was Laura Pelletier on the slab. They'd known each other since they were kids."

What did this mean to my case? I'd guessed that Laura was working with the Cabal but now it turned out that the woman I'd spoken with this morning wasn't Laura at all.

Christina must have guessed from my silence what I was thinking. "I'd say that the person you know as Laura Pelletier is actually—"

"A changeling," I said.

"Yeah."

All the pieces fit. The month long absence, the change in personality, the nocturnal wandering. Changelings—shape-shifting creatures from Faerie—assumed the form of someone else but they had to keep the victim's body close for a full lunar cycle, during which time they fed on its energy at night. Laura hadn't been sneaking out of her building because she was a werewolf, as one over-imaginative neighbor had assumed, but because she was going to the real Laura Pelletier's body and slowly draining it.

"Looks like my case just re-opened," Christina said. "Your colleague said you're in Maine? I'm coming over there."

"You don't have to do that," I told her. "I have everything under control here. I'll deal with it."

"I do have to," she said. "Thanks to my incompetent assistant, my official case report says I let a changeling get away. I can't have that on my record."

I wasn't sure I wanted another P.I. poking her nose into my case but I understood her need to put things right. "Okay, but things here are a little more complicated than just taking out a changeling."

"Fine," she said. "Give me the details when I get there. I don't want to step all over your case but the changeling is mine, okay? I can't believe I let her slip through my fingers."

"The woman you were following turned up dead. No one can blame you for closing the case."

"I blame myself," she said. "Text me your location and I'll get a flight."

"Okay, I'll do that."

"And don't go killing anything until I get there." She ended the call.

I texted her the details of the Lake Shore Lodge and she replied with a smiley-faced emoji.

Leon brought two mugs of coffee over to the table. "What was that all about?"

I told him and he listened with rapt attention. When I was done, he said, "A changeling, huh? Like those creatures that tried to kill my friend James and his girlfriend?"

"Exactly the same," I said, recalling the case I'd been working on when Leon and I had first met. "The Cabal must have replaced the real Laura Pelletier so that the changeling version could convince Dan to send Cathy to Butterfly Heights. After seeing what Cathy could do, they wanted her to become part of the project they're running up there."

Leon frowned. "So why didn't they just

replace Dan with a changeling? That sounds a lot easier to me."

I thought about that for a moment. "They couldn't replace Dan because during the first month of a changeling taking on someone's identity, it hasn't acquired all the traits of its victim. The Cabal probably surmised that Cathy —having faerie blood—would recognize what the changeling actually was and might escape through another rift."

I took a sip of the coffee. Leon was right, I did need it. "By replacing Laura while she was miles away and letting the changeling gradually take over her identity in New York, the Cabal was alleviating that problem. By the time changeling-Laura returned, she'd be fully integrated into her new identity and there'd be less chance of Cathy seeing her for what she really was."

"That makes sense, I guess. And once Cathy was a patient at Butterfly Heights, the Cabal had no more use for Dan so he was killed." He held up a hand, stopping me before I could reply. "No, wait a minute. That ritual in the cave, the one with the long-ass name. That puts the life essence of the victim into a jar. The blood and all that stuff. Dan is Cathy's dad so it stands to reason that he also has the Walker of Worlds power in his genes. That's how Cathy got it; it's been passed down through generations, right?"

"Right," I said.

"The ritual allows them to make a faerie creature from the blood and guts in the jar. In the case of Dan Pelletier's blood and guts, whatever creature they make from that will have the rift power."

I nodded. "I was thinking the same thing."

He furrowed his brow. "But like you said, there are plenty of ways to get from one realm to another so why is this rift stuff so important to the Cabal?"

That question was the sticking point in my understanding of what the Cabal was up to. "I don't know," I admitted.

"So what's our next move? Shouldn't we just storm Butterfly Heights and rescue Cathy from the Cabal?"

That actually wasn't such a bad idea. Whatever operation the Cabal was running needed to be shut down. Cathy seemed to be valuable to that operation—they'd gone to a lot of trouble to get her to the Heights—and needed to be removed from there as soon as possible.

"There's someone else we need to rescue as well," I told him, pointing at the drawing of Lydia Cornell sitting in a prison cell.

"Of course. So should we find out where Merlin is hiding and get him involved?"

"Why?"

"Taking down the Cabal was the promise you made to the Lady of the Lake, remember? And

Merlin has Excalibur, which you're supposed to use to do the job."

"I don't want to touch that sword ever again. It drains my energy and then feeds it back to me later when I'm weak. When I take down the Cabal, it will be without the sword."

He held up his hands. "No argument from me. You know I don't trust Merlin. And it sounds like the sword is corrupt. Things didn't end well for King Arthur, after all." He sipped his coffee. "So it's just me, you, and the P.I. from New York against the Cabal?"

"We can't really rely on Christina Flores," I said. "She's only coming here for the changeling. We're gonna need more help," I said. "Society protocol states that if a P.I. discovers an enemy enclave, then its location has to be reported to the Shadow Watch."

"Ugh! Fuck those guys."

"Yeah, and the protocol was written a long time ago, before the Society was infiltrated by Cabal spies. If we report this, someone will probably warn the Cabal that we're coming."

He nodded. "So who do we trust? I can get Michael involved."

"Of course."

"The Blackwell sisters? They're pretty handy in a fight."

"We can ask them."

"What about Mallory and Tia? I'm sure the

sorceress has some tricks up her sleeve and Mallory is a good fighter. Hell, she cut off Rekhmire's arm."

So we had ourselves plus five—possibly six if Christina decided to join—other people to take on two Cabal strongholds. The people on our team were strong but there was no way the numbers worked in our favor. There could be hundreds, or even thousands, of Cabal members. Gloria had said the organization was using Faerie to prepare for war against the Society so I had to assume that the castle where Lydia was being held was full of enemy soldiers.

Maybe I had no choice but to get the Shadow Watch involved, even though to do so was risky. There just didn't seem to be any other option.

"You know what's sad?" Leon said.

"What?"

"The list of team members is severely lacking without Felicity on it."

"Yeah, I know. Maybe I should call Michael Chester and see if he's unearthed anything regarding her whereabouts."

He nodded. "Wouldn't hurt to ask."

I called the Society headquarters in London and told the switchboard operator I wanted to speak to Michael Chester. After the call was put through, Michael answered his phone quickly. "Hello." He didn't say my name, although he would know it was me thanks to the magical caller ID system at headquarters.

"Michael, it's Alec," I said redundantly. "I was just wondering if you've found anything about—"

"Yes," he said, cutting me off. "Yes, I have. I can't discuss that matter over the phone right now." His voice sounded odd, as if someone might be standing in the room with him.

"Oh," I said. "So will you call me back when it's more convenient?"

"No, no, I can't do that. You're going to have to give me a location."

"You want to speak face to face?"

"It's the only way I'm afraid."

I hesitated. My last encounter with members of the Society had involved me being interrogated with a Collar of Truth around my neck. How did I know Michael wasn't going to turn up here with a truckload of agents who wanted to question me further about the Melandra Codex? The last thing I needed right now was for them to complicate matters.

"Alec, I know where you live and work so there shouldn't be any issue with simply telling me where you are," he said in my ear in a tone so low that it was almost a whisper. Then he added, "This is important. I have news regarding two people very close to you."

One of those people must be Felicity but who was the second? Oh yeah, my father. I gave

Michael the location of the Greenville Mall. I had no reason to lead him right to my front door.

His voice lowered even further. "Be there in thirty minutes."

"I will," I said as I ended the call.

"Trouble?" Leon asked.

"Maybe. We're going to meet Michael Chester at the mall. He says he has information regarding Felicity and possibly my dad."

"Your dad? He's been missing a while."

I shrugged. "It sounds like Michael found him."

"Okay," he said, finishing his coffee. "What are we waiting for? Let's go."

It took us twenty minutes to get to the mall and by the time we arrived, the rain had started to come down again. At the moment, it was little more than an insidious drizzle but the dark clouds that were rolling in from the north threatened to increase that drizzle to a downpour.

I parked the Land Rover in a space that was some distance from any other cars. If something went down here, I didn't want a member of the public wandering into the middle of it.

We got out and selected a sword and dagger each from the trunk before getting back into the vehicle. I had no reason to believe Michael was going to appear with hostile forces but I also had no reason to disbelieve it either. The man had been my father's secretary and that should count for something, I supposed, but my dad had been missing awhile now and seemed to have abandoned the Society completely. So Michael's association with him didn't really stand him in good stead.

"How is he going to get here from London in half an hour?" Leon mused as he watched the rain fall over the parking lot.

"Some sort of portal, I guess. See, that's what I mean about portals; there are hundreds of different magic items that open them so why is a Walker of Worlds so important to the Cabal? We've established it isn't just for her faerie genes. They want her to be able to use her power. Why?" Not knowing the answer to that question was frustrating.

"Don't ask me," he said, "I'm just the IT guy." He grinned at me.

Before I could reply, a sound like thunder sounded across the parking lot and the air there flashed for a split second, like a camera flash but a thousand time brighter. "I think he's here," I said to Leon as I tried to blink away the bright spots that had appeared in my vision.

A man I assumed to be Michael Chester was standing in the parking lot where the air had torn open. He was a short man with a balding head, drooping mustache, and wire-framed glasses. He wore a light blue dress shirt, black trousers, and a tan sports jacket. He adjusted the glasses with one hand and looked around the parking lot desperately.

I opened my door and got out, waving to him.

He spotted me and ran in the direction of the Land Rover.

"Why is he running?" Leon asked.

"I don't know but it probably isn't good."

Michael was waving me back inside the car. "Start the engine!" he shouted. "They followed me!"

The air behind him burst into a series of flashes, as if a hundred photographers had just spotted a famous star on the red carpet. At least a dozen figures appeared in the parking lot, dressed in black and armed with glowing blue enchanted swords.

I got behind the wheel and started the Land Rover before flooring the gas and speeding through the parking lot toward Michael.

When I reached him, I hit the brakes and shouted, "Get in!"

The Land Rover skidded to a stop. Michael wrenched open the rear door and threw himself into the vehicle. I spun the steering wheel and hit the gas again, sending us rocketing toward the exit.

Leon had turned in his seat and was watching our pursuers through the rear window. "They're getting cars," he said.

I nodded grimly. In the rearview mirror, I could see the dozen or so figures split into pairs and approach various parked cars in the lot. As they got close to a car, its doors opened and its engine started. They had some sort of car-jacking magical item I'd never seen before.

Michael was sitting up in the back seat now, panting like crazy.

"What's happening?" I asked him as six cars peeled away from their parking spaces and chased after us.

"I found out about their operation to capture your father and now they're trying to kill me," he said.

"Operation? What operation?"

"Operation Prophecy," he said. "Get us out of here and I'll tell you all about it."

15

The rain had become a downpour now as we sped north along the highway, with six cars in pursuit. The highway was busy and as we weaved around the traffic, I realized that if we stayed on this road, the likelihood of a crash was high, especially in this weather. I needed to get us off the highway and somewhere more remote to protect the innocent drivers on this road.

Up ahead, I saw a turn off that led away from the highway and through farmland. When I reached it, I hit the brakes momentarily and spun the wheel. The Land Rover fishtailed for a split second and then we were on the narrower road that led through the fields.

"What's our plan?" Leon asked me from the passenger seat.

"If you have one, I'd like to hear it."

"I don't but we can't keep running forever.

We'll run out of gas or they'll catch up with us eventually."

He was right. At some point, we were going to have to stand and fight.

"And now the police are on our tail," Leon added, pointing back at the highway where a patrol car was racing toward the rear of the pack of cars behind us, lights flashing and siren blaring.

Our pursuers weren't about to stop and get a ticket; they seemed oblivious to the patrol car and focused only on catching up with us.

"Michael, can you handle a sword?" I asked the man in the backseat.

He looked nervous at the suggestion. "Well, I took an hour of mandatory training once but my job doesn't really demand physical prowess."

"I'll take that as a no." I looked at Leon. "Looks like it's me and you against twelve of them."

He nodded solemnly. "I don't like those odds."

"Maybe I can find a place where we can use the terrain or a building to our advantage. Taking them all on at once probably won't end well but if we can negate the advantage their superior numbers give them, we might have a chance."

"We may not have a choice," Michael said, pointing through the back window.

The passenger in the car directly behind us —a white Toyota—was hanging out of his window and pointing something at us. The item in his hand looked like a wand made of white stone.

"You're going to want to get out of the way of that," Michael advised.

I jerked the wheel to the right and the Land Rover responded by taking us off the road and crashing through a wooden fence into a cornfield. As we cut through the crop, stalks and leaves smashed against the vehicle.

The section of the road we'd just left exploded with blue light as the wand-like item discharged. The road had become a dangerous place thanks to the wand wielder but I couldn't stay in the cornfield forever because the plants were slowing us down. Our pursuers were still on the road, parallel with us now, the patrol car doggedly following them with its lights flashing.

The guy with the wand took aim at us.

I had no way to avoid the blast that was about to come shooting in our direction. I couldn't outrun it either because of the thick corn stalks slapping against the Land Rover and getting under the wheels.

"Brace yourselves," I said.

The blast from the wand was silent but the air around the Land Rover flashed with a blue so vivid and bright that I thought I might be blinded by it. As well as the light, there was some sort of force that rushed under the vehicle and sent it—

along with corn stalks, leaves, and husks—
hurtling into the blue-tinged air.

The vehicle flipped over twice and I felt my
stomach lurch as the world beyond the
windshield spun crazily. When we finally hit the
ground, I felt a jolt slam through every bone in
my body. The airbags deployed just as my head
was thrown forward, cushioning my skull and
preventing it from being smashed on the
dashboard and my brains becoming corn
chowder.

The Land Rover came to a stop on its roof,
still spinning slightly as I fumbled for my
seatbelt. "Is everyone okay?" I asked. My voice
sounded distant and muffled, as if it didn't belong
to me at all.

"Yeah," Leon said. He didn't sound okay; his
voice sounded distant and muffled too.

"Michael?" I asked. My seatbelt disengaged
and I fell to the floor, which was actually the roof.

"I'll live, I think," he said groggily.

"We have to get out of here," I said. "They'll be
coming. Where are the swords?" Miraculously,
we'd been in a spinning vehicle with two swords
and daggers and no one had been killed. Equally
miraculously, my door opened when I pulled on
the handle. The miracles ended there, though,
because I had no idea where the swords and
daggers had gone. I was about to face a dozen
enemies with my bare hands.

There was my magic, of course, but my head felt so muddled that I couldn't bring any of the magic circles into my mind's eye and without them I couldn't do anything.

Using the upturned Land Rover as a balance aid, I managed to get my feet and stand unsteadily in the circular clearing the wand blast had created in the cornfield. The ground was slick and wet and more rain hissed down all around me, splashing against the rows of corn and the underside of the Land Rover.

The enemies were coming. Their cars were on the road, doors open, with no occupants. Everyone was making his or her way through the corn to this location. The patrol car had also stopped and its lights were still flashing but the siren, thankfully, had been turned off. The officer had vacated the vehicle. He was a hell of an optimist if he was following those guys through the corn, thinking he was going to serve tickets to the drivers of the vehicles. I just prayed he didn't get hurt.

The twelve men emerged from the corn and stood at the edge of the clearing. Apart from the guy with the wand, they all wielded glowing swords.

I became dimly aware of Leon standing behind me.

"Do you have a weapon?" I asked him. Why was my voice still muffled and distant?

"No," he said. "I couldn't find them. Maybe they got thrown out of the car."

"Better that than thrown into us," I said.

"Yeah, you've got to look on the bright side." He lifted his arm slowly and pointed at the dozen guys at the edge of the clearing. "Why are they trying to kill us again?"

"So we don't find out about Operation Prophecy."

"Oh, yeah." He frowned. "What's Operation Prophecy again?"

"We don't know yet."

"Ah."

"We have to keep Michael alive so he can tell us."

He nodded slowly. "Got it."

The men advanced as one, as if an invisible commander had given them the order.

"Here they come," Leon said.

"Yeah, I see that."

He lifted his fists like a boxer. I did the same.

I didn't think much of our chances.

"Now would be a good time for one of those magic blasts," Leon suggested.

I shook my head. "Can't do it."

"Damn. I thought you were waiting until the last minute to make it more dramatic."

"I wish I were." I tried to picture one of the magic circles in my head but they weren't cooperating.

The twelve men had halved the distance between them and us.

"Why don't they just blast us with the wand?" Leon whispered to me, as if scared that the men might hear him and get ideas.

"They're probably going to interrogate us before they kill us."

"Oh, so we get to live a little longer. That's nice."

"Believe me, it won't be nice."

The police officer emerged from the trees, striding purposefully toward the men he'd been chasing.

"If he's going to arrest them, now would be a good time," Leon said. The twelve would be on us in a matter of seconds.

"Alec," the police officer said.

I looked over at him, wondering how he knew my name, and he tossed something to me. I realized it was a sword as it flew toward me. When I caught it by the handle and felt a surge of raw power flood my being, I realized it was Excalibur.

All of the pain and grogginess I'd experienced from the crash vanished in an instant. I felt superhumanly strong. A memory came to me from a Saturday morning cartoon; He-Man holding aloft his Sword of Power and crying out, "I have the power!" That was how I felt right now. I had the power.

Instead of waiting for the twelve enemies to reach us, I sprang forward, slashing Excalibur in front of me in a horizontal arc. The element of surprise was on my side and the five men who dropped to the ground, blood spurting from various arteries, had looks of shock on their faces as they died.

Even more power rushed from the sword into my arm and then into every part of me. Why had I ever tried to deny this weapon? Why had I ever resisted it? I must have been a fool.

The guy with the wand raised it against me. It wasn't the smartest decision because Excalibur slashed down and parted his forearm from his upper arm at the elbow. He screamed but the sound was cut off when the sword sliced through his neck. His body, now in three parts, lay on the ground at my feet.

With half their number gone, the remaining six would-be attackers looked at one another nervously, as if silently daring each other to attack me.

I didn't wait to see who was going to take the dare. I thrust Excalibur's sharp tip into the chest of the man closest to me and withdrew it quickly so I could use it to block a blade that was arcing toward my head. The two swords clashed and after deflecting the attack, I thrust Excalibur into the neck of the attacker. He went down, gurgling and choking.

The four remaining men came at me as one, their swords whirling and flashing. The air was filled with the clang of metal and a shower of sparks as five blades met each other. One of those blades was a powerful sword of legend and it shattered the others so that the four attackers were left holding broken, useless pieces of metal.

Excalibur took charge and slashed this way and that until the four men joined their eight companions lying on the ground in the clearing.

The sword was still sending energy through me, as if it had cut out the life essences of the twelve men and was giving them to me as a gift. I closed my eyes and let the power course through me. I felt as if I could enter Butterfly Heights alone and single-handedly take on everyone in there and then do the same at the Cabal's castle in Faerie. With each kill would come more and more power until I'd be invincible.

"Alec?" Leon asked. "What just happened?"

I opened my eyes. Michael was out of the Land Rover now, his eyes darting nervously over the twelve dead men on the ground.

"What happened," Merlin said, approaching us, "Is that Alec finally did what he was supposed to be doing all along; using Excalibur to destroy the Cabal."

"These men aren't Cabal members," Michael said. "They're members of the Society. At least I think they are."

I surveyed the carnage in the clearing. I'd killed men who were supposed to be on my side. They were allies, not enemies.

Leon put his hands on my shoulders and looked into my eyes. "Hey, whatever you're thinking right now, get it out of your head. These guys were going to kill us. You saved my life, and Michael's too."

"Yes, you did," Michael said. "These men may be part of the Society but they belong to a splinter group that conducts its own secret operations, actions not sanctioned by the Society."

I let go of Excalibur, letting it fall to the ground. Merlin's face became concerned when he saw that. He walked over to me and said, "Don't worry about any of this, Alec. We can fix this in a matter of seconds."

He raised his arms, palms facing the Land Rover. He rotated his wrists and the vehicle rose from the ground, spinning lazily in the air so that it was the right way up. Merlin lowered his arms and my car descended slowly until the tires gently touched the ground.

It may be back on its tires again but the Land Rover had taken a beating. Most of the windows were broken, the bodywork was crushed in places, and pieces of the engine lay scattered in the cornfield.

Merlin closed his eyes and said a few words

under his breath. The broken glass shards flew together and melded into unblemished pieces of glass. The airbags deflated and were sucked back into their places in the dash. The dents and holes in the bodywork repaired themselves as if being fixed by invisible hands.

The scattered pieces of engine skittered across the ground to the vehicle and shot into their proper places. By the time Merlin's spell was complete, the Land Rover looked brand new.

"Wow," Leon said to the wizard. "I know who to call the next time I have a fender-bender."

"Now you three be on your way," Merlin said, "While I deal with these bodies."

I wasn't going to argue with that; Officer Davis already had his suspicions about me. If a dozen bodies turned up in a cornfield, he'd be hounding me before the corpses were even identified.

Leaving Excalibur on the ground, I climbed into the Land Rover. The engine started first time and purred like a waking lion.

I wound down my window and said to Merlin, "What are you going to do with them?"

"Don't worry, Alec," he said matter-of-factly, "They'll never ever be found."

His answer made me realize I probably didn't want to know the details. I drove slowly through the corn and back through the hole the Land Rover had made in the fence earlier.

When we got on the road, I turned the wheel in the direction of the Lodge and looked at Michael in the rearview mirror. He was still shaken.

"I need to know why I just had to kill twelve men," I said. "What the hell is Operation Prophecy?"

16

"Operation Prophecy," Michael said, "is something I stumbled upon while trying to determine Felicity's whereabouts."

We were at the cabin now, sitting on the plastic chairs beneath the porch roof while Michael paced back and forth along the porch's edge. During the drive from the cornfield, he'd gradually become more anxious and now there seemed to be a shot of nervous adrenaline running through his body.

That was understandable; I assumed his job at the Society of Shadows headquarters involved sitting at a desk. The most dangerous task he performed in his line of work was probably refilling the coffee machine. Now, he'd narrowly avoided being killed by a magical energy bolt, a car crash, and a dozen deadly killers.

"The files were hidden but I've been working

with the Society's computer system for so long, I know how to reveal most of its secrets. I teased them out gradually—one by one—and what I discovered shocked me." He turned to me and said, "As you know, your father disappeared. In fact, I'm the one who broke the news to you when you called me some months ago."

I remembered the call. I'd been in Canada at the time, working with my friend Jim Walker. That had been when Gloria was still alive and an exile from Faerie because the Cabal had invaded her homeland.

"A certain element of the Society wanted to find Thomas," Michael continued. "They discovered that he'd stolen a scroll called the Melandra Codex a number of years ago and they wanted it back. They initiated Operation Prophecy in an effort to find him and recover the Codex. The methods they employed are quite frightening. I'm not even sure how they managed it. The files I read didn't contain all the details."

"What do you know for certain?" I asked.

He stopped pacing for a moment and looked at us with a grave expression. "They couldn't find Thomas by any of the usual means—he seemed to have disappeared off the face of the Earth—so they used a witch who had the gift of Prophecy to make predictions regarding his whereabouts in the future."

"So they could turn up at that place and time and capture him," Leon said.

Michael nodded. "Yes, that was their plan. That's what Operation Prophecy was all about. But there are a couple of things about their methods that are highly disturbing."

He hugged himself as if against the cold and looked out over the lake. "Highly disturbing indeed," he half-whispered.

"Like what?" I asked.

"First of all, you need to understand how the gift of Prophecy works," he said. "Only a very few witches can prophesy anything at all and even then, the results are usually extremely vague. Events of wide-reaching importance can be prophesied with greater accuracy than lesser events, which is why fortune tellers can't really tell anyone their future; there just aren't any events in a person's life that are important enough to become part of a prophecy."

He began pacing again. "So it's strange that they consulted a witch in the first place. They must have thought that something was going to happen in Thomas Harbinger's life that would be a big enough event to trigger a prophecy. Why did they believe that? Because the Melandra Codex is so powerful that if your father had it, whatever he was going to do with it would be something huge."

"That makes sense," Leon said.

Yes, it sounds logical," Michael said. "But they were wrong. The prophecy that was given to the splinter group was that Thomas Harbinger would meet with Felicity Lake in England. It had nothing to do with the Melandra Codex."

I frowned, confused. My dad meeting Felicity didn't exactly sound earth shattering. "What kind of half-ass prophecy is that?"

"I know it doesn't sound like much but your father meeting Felicity was a momentous enough occasion to generate a prophecy."

I shook my head. "I'm not buying it. They've met plenty of times before and nothing earth-shattering happened."

"But *this* time," Michael said, "the meeting was important." He stopped pacing and finally sat down on the edge of the porch. "The thing that worries me the most is that the witch gave a list of possible dates and times when the meeting could take place."

Leon leaned forward in his chair. "That's very specific. I thought you said prophecies are always vague."

"They are. The future is changeable and probabilities shift all the time. I've never heard of a witch powerful enough to give a prophecy with specific dates."

"But these guys work for the Society, right? So the powerful witch is also working for the Society."

"The splinter group consists of Society members," Michael said. "But they may be traitors. They might have teamed up with the Cabal. I don't know."

Leon raised an eyebrow. "So if those guys were traitors, that means there's some sort of super-witch working for the Cabal."

Michael nodded gravely. "Yes, it means exactly that."

That was all we needed. While the Society seemed to be getting weaker through in-fighting and infiltration by its enemies, the Midnight Cabal was growing in power. Not only was it running some sort of global pharmaceutical company, it also had a powerful witch providing its members with deadly accurate prophecies.

As far as I knew, the Society still didn't know that the Cabal had taken over some parts of Faerie in preparation for a war. Who could I tell? Who could I trust? With my father missing from the Society's ranks, I had no one to turn to.

"The meeting between Felicity and Thomas went ahead," Michael said. "The splinter group, Cabal traitors—whatever you want to call them— tried to capture Thomas but failed. He got away and took Felicity with him. I believe the witch is being consulted again to provide a further prophecy that might lead to his capture."

"And meanwhile, they found out you'd

uncovered Operation Prophecy and chased you here," I guessed.

"Yes, I obviously set off some sort of digital—or magical—security they'd placed on their files." He looked out over the lake sadly. "Traitors and spies have corrupted the Society. The entire organization is crumbling. I can't go back."

"What will you do?" I asked.

"I've been working on a fallback plan for a while now. I saw the writing on the wall a long time ago and although I never wanted this day to arrive, I'm prepared for it."

"You have somewhere to go?"

He nodded. "Somewhere they'll never find me. In fact, I should probably leave before they realize the guys who came after me failed and they send someone else."

"You need a ride anywhere?"

He shook his head and held up a small emerald. "My travel arrangements are already made. It was nice meeting you and thanks for saving my life. When you see your father, give him my regards." He squeezed his fist around the gemstone and disappeared in a sudden bright green flash.

"Well that was short and sweet," Leon said.

"And worrying. If there's a witch as powerful as Michael suggested, it can only mean trouble."

He sighed. "Yeah, the Cabal seems to be holding all the killer cards. A super-witch.

Rekhmire. Who knows what else it has up its sleeve?"

"I'm sure we'll find out soon enough."

"What was that stuff about Felicity meeting your dad? Why would that be significant enough to warrant a prophecy?"

I shrugged and said, "I have no idea. I guess that whatever they're doing together, it must be something important."

"This building is where the you'll be housed," Thomas Harbinger said, taking Felicity along a flagstone path that led away from the main academy building to a smaller structure. "I'll show you around and let you get settled in before we embark on our first mission."

"Mission?" Everything was happening so fast that Felicity felt as if she'd hardly had time to think. Was she expected to live here now? In this realm far away from everyone she knew? What about her friends and family? She couldn't just disappear.

"I'll explain about the mission in due course," Thomas said as they reached the door of the smaller building. He was about to press his hand against the decorated wood—the carvings on this door featured Jason and the Argonauts on the deck of the *Argo*, fighting the Stymphalian Birds with swords and spears—but then stopped and said, "This door will only open for you. Just press your hand here."

She did as she was asked and the door swung inward.

"Much better than a keycard," Thomas said, grinning. He gestured at the open door and Felicity went through. She found herself standing in what looked like a communal lounge; a large, high-ceilinged space with comfortable looking sofas and chairs, a huge stone fireplace, and side tables with lamps sitting on them. Bookshelves had been built into one long wall and they were filled with all kinds of books from leather-bound tomes to paperbacks.

"Your own library," Thomas said. "There's a bedroom, office, spare rooms, and a bathroom upstairs. I'm sure you'll find it to your liking."

When he'd said she'd be housed here, Felicity had assumed she'd have a room here but that the rest of the building—like the huge lounge— would be shared with other members of staff. But if the place only had one bedroom...

"Are you saying this entire building is my quarters?"

Thomas nodded. "Yes, of course. This will be your residence. You're welcome to have a house on the Earthly realm as well, if you want, but while you're in this realm, this is all yours."

Felicity let her eyes wander over the space, which could easily house a dozen people. "But it's so large. What about the other members of staff? Where will they live?"

"There are other buildings like this on the campus," he said. "There's no shortage of space in this realm. We're the only ones here."

With perks like this, Thomas wasn't going to have any trouble getting people to work at Harbinger Academy.

"The only downside is that there's no cell reception," he said with a chuckle. "At least we won't have to tell the students to put their phones away. Now, I'll let you get acquainted with your new home while I attend to a few things in my office. Just come over to the main building when you're ready and we'll begin our first task."

"All right," she said, wondering if the bathroom had a shower. After her sudden flight from Manchester and hours spent in Thomas's Land Rover, it would be good to freshen up.

"I'll leave you to it, then." He exited via the front door, which closed behind him seemingly by itself.

Felicity ascended the wide stairs to the first floor. She found the office first, a generous room equipped with a wide desk, more books, and a plush dark blue sofa that sat beneath an arched window. The view from the window showed the other buildings and the woods beyond. The trees seemed to reach all the way to the horizon. Just how big was this realm?

The room next door was a bedroom of roughly the same dimensions as Felicity's entire house in Dearmont. Another arched window looked out over the campus and the light streaming in through the window illuminated a large, comfortable-looking bed. There was also a fireplace in here and a seating area furnished with armchairs, a long coffee table, and more bookshelves.

Built-in closets provided more space than Felicity would ever need for clothes.

She discovered the bathroom across the hallway and immediately realized that mentally questioning whether her new residence would have a shower had been ridiculous. The room—which was lit by light diffusing in through frosted windows set high in the walls—was like a professional health spa.

The floor was fashioned from smooth stone flagstones, the walls covered with tiny tiles that formed a mosaic of a lagoon on one wall and the interior of a cave with a glowing pool in its center on another.

A set of tiled steps led up to a hot tub and a conventional bathtub—which looked large enough in which to swim—sat beneath the frosted windows. A marble counter ran along one wall with two sinks built into its surface and a long mirror on the wall behind it. The far corner of the room was equipped with a variety of nozzles that far surpassed Felicity's need for a simple shower. A set of dove gray towels waited on a rail near the counter, along with a white bathrobe.

A plain stone door led to a smaller room that contained a toilet and another sink.

If this residence was typical of what Thomas Harbinger was offering to the teaching staff at the academy, he wasn't going to have any problems finding and keeping personnel.

Felicity undressed and placed her clothes on the marble counter before walking naked into the shower area. The console that controlled the nozzles and water flow was nothing like anything she'd seen before. It seemed more like a stone tablet than anything else. Numbers and diagrams had been carved into the stone and after a minute of inspection, Felicity had worked out which carvings indicated temperature and which controlled the showerheads.

She worked out a combination of buttons to press and soon found out that the carvings weren't buttons at all; she only had to hold her finger above them and they glowed blue, indicating that they'd been activated.

The nozzles came to life and sprayed hot

water from various directions. Felicity let her muscles relax, enjoying the sensation of the water playing over her skin. She let her mind wander over recent events and the prophecy she'd been informed of by the Coven.

If Harbinger Academy was humanity's last hope, as the witches and Thomas had suggested it was, then she wanted desperately to be a part of that. The only thing that didn't sit comfortably with her was not being able to tell Alec about the end-times prophecy. He was still working for the Society of Shadows, which was riddled with traitors and slowly crumbling. Surely he should be warned about his own employers.

She'd promised not to tell, though, and the dire warnings of the witches were enough incentive to make sure she kept that promise.

Besides, Alec was smart; he'd figure out the situation regarding the Society soon enough and somehow extricate himself from it before the whole thing collapsed.

A bar of soap and a small bottle of shampoo sat on a small stone shelf next to the shower console. Felicity used them to wash away the perspiration and dirt she felt she'd accumulated since going on the run from the Society and then waved her hand at the stone tablet to turn off the water.

As she donned the bathrobe, she felt more

invigorated than she would after a regular shower and wondered if the water, or the shower itself, held some sort of magical rejuvenation properties.

She was surprised to find her suitcase sitting inside the bathroom door. The last time she'd seen it had been in her house in Manchester. Obviously the witches were taking care of her relocation arrangements and had somehow magicked the case here.

After selecting fresh clothes from the case—a pair of jeans and a white turtleneck sweater—she took the case to her bedroom and placed it beside the bed, wondering if the witches would be able to get hold of the rest of her clothes; the ones she'd packed in boxes for the Society to ship to Manchester from Dearmont.

That question was answered when—on impulse—she opened the closet and found the rest of her clothes hanging there.

She was even more surprised when she went downstairs and out of the front door and found her Mini parked outside the building.

Thomas was standing beside it with a grin on his face. "How's that for an efficient moving service? You should find everything else you own in your spare rooms. As for the Society, they're going to wonder where the hell all this stuff went to when the ship docks in England. Is everything okay with your residence? If there's anything you'd like to change—"

"It's perfect," Felicity said.

"Good. Then let's begin our first mission. Come on, we'll use one of the lecture halls." He walked over to the main building and Felicity followed.

Once onside, he took her along a corridor and through a door that led into a lecture hall that looked like it might belong inside any educational facility. Semi-circular rows of benches descended to a stage where a lectern had been set up along with a whiteboard and a screen.

Thomas went down to the stage and told Felicity to make herself comfortable. She took a seat on the second row and waited to hear about the mission she'd be undertaking.

"We know that at some point in the future, the realms are going to spill into each other," Thomas began. "At that time, mankind will be vulnerable to the paranormal creatures that cross over into the Earthly realm. Harbinger Academy exists so that we can train a new order of protectors who will be skilled in magical arts that have all but vanished in the mists of time."

Felicity nodded. She was here to be a part of that training.

"But before the realms spill into each other," Thomas said, "there will be a period of time when the Earthly realm will be completely cut off from all magic."

"When the Melandra Configuration spell is used to save the world," Felicity added.

Thomas nodded. "When the Melandra Configuration is cast, all magic will cease to exist. Even the most basic magical item will become nothing more than a hunk of junk. The Earthly realm will be cut off from all the others. We don't know how long this will last before it is reversed and the spill occurs."

"That's the part I don't understand," she told him. "If the Earthly realm is cut off from all the others and magic disappears, isn't that what we've been fighting for all this time? For humans to live without the threat of paranormal danger?"

"Yes, it is."

"So why will that situation be reversed at all? Can't we prevent that from happening? Then we can stop the realms from spilling into each other and live happily ever after."

"That sounds ideal, I grant you," he said, going to the whiteboard, "but the reversal will occur to save mankind, just as the Melandra Configuration will be cast for exactly the same reason." He picked up a marker and drew a blue circle on the whiteboard. To its right, he drew a green circle of the same size and to its left, a larger black circle.

"This is Earth in the middle," he said, pointing

at the blue circle. "At the moment, there are doorways from there to the Faerie realm." He added dots to the diagram, connecting the blue and green circles. "And to the Shadow Land." He added more dots to connect the blue and black circles. "And between Faerie and Shadow Land." Placing more dots on the whiteboard, he connected all the circles.

"Not to mention various other realms such as the one we are in now," he said, drawing a dozen smaller circles on the board. "This is the way things have always been. There is some movement between the realms but it is limited, as the doorways between Earth, Faerie, and the Shadow Land are few and mostly hidden. Now, here's something you may not know; the Midnight Cabal has been taking over parts of Faerie as part of its war effort against the Society."

"Yes, I know that," Felicity said. "Alec discovered that some time ago when he helped Gloria...I mean the Lady of the Forest. She'd been kicked out of her home by Cabal invaders."

His face fell. "Oh, you already knew."

"Alec called the Society to let you know what was happening but you'd disappeared and he didn't know who else he could trust with the information."

"Oh, I see. Well, anyway, here's the Cabal." He scribbled a black square into the green circle that represented Faerie. "They plan to use a portal from Faerie to attack the Society, probably by stepping through it into the Society's headquarters and assassinating everyone inside. Such a blow would destroy the Society. But the plan has a flaw; the headquarters building is shielded from magical attacks."

"So their plan can't work," Felicity said.

"Not if they try to use a magical item or a spell." He used the green marker to write Walker of Worlds over the Faerie circle. "Have you heard of these creatures?"

Remembering her folklore, Felicity nodded. "They're an extremely rare type of Faerie being that can open portals between realms."

"And they don't need magic to do it," Thomas added. "They possess a skill that allows them to cross the barriers between worlds using their minds. There's no magic involved. I don't know how the physics works exactly but I do know that the Cabal has been searching for a Walker so it can carry out its attack on the Society HQ. The building is protected from magical portals but any portal created by a Walker of Worlds isn't magical."

"So the Cabal could circumvent the Society's defenses." The thought of such a large-scale slaughter made her shiver. How many people would die if the Cabal managed to enter the building by surprise?

"Yes, it could," Thomas said. "Now, add to that the fact that all magic is going to be turned off for a while. There will be no way to cross to or from the Earthly realm using any kind of magical item or spell."

"So if the Cabal has a Walker in its employ, it will have a huge advantage," Felicity finished for him. "Only its members will be able to pass between realms."

"Exactly. The doors between realms will be locked to everyone else but the Cabal will have a skeleton key to unlock any of them it cares to. We can't allow that to happen, can we?"

"No, it would be a disaster. The Cabal would be able to run roughshod over everything in its way."

"Yes, it would," Thomas said. "And it intends to. Its members know the prophecy about magic disappearing so they've been desperately trying to locate a Walker of Worlds to get the upper hand when that event occurs. Unfortunately, they've found one."

Felicity felt suddenly cold. "That's terrible."

"It is. But the girl they've found didn't know she had the ability to open portals and is in a state of shock after doing it accidentally. The Cabal doctors haven't been able to get through to her. We need to rescue her before they find a way to control her and her powers."

"All right," she said. "What do we need to do?"

"The girl is in a place called Butterfly Heights. We need to break in and—"

"Butterfly Heights?"

He nodded. "Yes."

"Alec and I worked a case there. We discovered it had been used by Cabal members in the '40s. They were carrying out some sort of genetic experiments there."

"Well it looks like they still are."

"So how are we going to get inside and get the girl out?"

He grinned. "We have a few methods at our disposal. We need to decide on one and formulate a plan."

"There's something else that's been bothering me," she said. "The Coven told us the prophecy about magic being turned off but you said the Cabal knows the prophecy as well. Did a traitor from the Society leak the information?"

Thomas's eyes became sad and he shook his head. "I wish that were the case. It's preferable to the reality of the situation. When you met the Coven earlier, did you notice a gap in their circle?"

Felicity recalled a mental image of the nine witches sitting in a circle around the pool. There had been a gap between two of them but she hadn't thought anything of it at the time.

"There used to be ten of them," Thomas said.

"The Coven was originally made up of ten members."

Felicity frowned, confused. So where was the missing member?

"A traitor didn't reveal the prophecy to our enemies," Thomas said. "They're getting their information direct from the source. The Cabal has the tenth witch."

1 8

Leon and I were sitting on the porch eating pizza when Christina Flores arrived. It was getting late in the day and the sun had all but disappeared beneath the horizon, staining the underside of the clouds a dull orange before it gave way to the night completely.

A blue Jeep Renegade stopped next to my Land Rover and a lithe woman dressed in a denim jacket, white T-shirt, and blue jeans got out. She grabbed a brown paper sack from the passenger seat and sprinted through the rain to the porch, keeping her long black hair from getting too wet.

"Hey," she said. "I brought Chinese but I see you went Italian."

"Pull up a chair and we'll share," I said. "You want a beer to wash it down with?

"Hell, yeah." She placed the sack on the plastic

table and took a seat before looking from Leon to me. "Which one of you is Alec?"

"That's me," I said, shaking her hand. Her grip was strong and confident.

Leon introduced himself as my colleague and they shook.

"Christina," she said. "Nice to meet you. I understand you guys can help me close the Laura Pelletier case."

"We can," Leon said. "Alec tells me you thought the case was closed already."

She nodded and accepted the bottle of beer I offered her. "Yeah, as far as I knew, Laura was dead. Well, technically, she is. The real Laura I mean. The thing that's walking around in her skin is something else entirely."

"And you want to kill it," I said.

She took a swallow of beer and said, "That's my job. And since my assistant screwed up the case file, I feel I have to make things right."

"Does your assistant do that often? Make mistakes, I mean." Leon asked.

Christina pursed her lips for a moment, obviously thinking how best to answer the question. Her hesitation said it all. She confirmed it when she said, "Maybe they aren't mistakes." She lowered her voice and added, "I don't really trust him, to be honest. The Society whisked my old assistant away to a new job and gave me this guy a couple months ago. I think he might have an ulterior motive that has nothing to do with assisting me in my job."

"What do you mean?" I asked, aware of the similarity between her situation and my own.

She leaned forward. "You've heard the rumors, right? That the Society is basically being run by spies and traitors? I think my new guy has been sent to keep an eye on me for some reason."

Leon looked at me and arched an eyebrow. "Sounds familiar."

Christina looked at me closely. "You too?"

"I don't know if it's the same but my assistant was whisked away recently and replaced with someone else." I didn't add that Felicity had been taken away to fulfill a prophecy so that the Society could attempt to capture my father. There was only so much craziness I was willing to lay at a stranger's door.

And as for Carlton, I didn't think he was spying on me for the Society. I may have had that suspicion when I first met him but not any longer. "I don't think my new guy is a spy, though," I said.

"Well you're lucky," Christina said, "I hear all these rumors about stuff happening in the organization. Theft, murder, betrayal. I even heard that the Midnight Cabal is back in business after hundreds of years. Can you believe that?"

Leon and I looked at each other.

"Actually, there's some truth to that," I said.

Christina's brown eyes widened. "What? Really?"

"Yeah. In fact, that's why we're here."

She looked at the growing shadows around the lake as if Cabal operatives were about to leap out at us and lowered her voice even further. "The Cabal is here? In this neck of the woods?"

I nodded.

She took a swig of beer. "Tell me more. This changeling case just got a hell of a lot more interesting."

I told her about the basics of the case from when Dan Pelletier hired me to when Laura Pelletier, aka the changeling, took us to Butterfly Heights.

"And you think the Cabal runs the place?" she asked. She'd listened with interest and now her eyes held a look that was equal parts shock and excitement.

I nodded. "We need to get Cathy out of there. She's a Walker of Worlds—"

"Whoa! A faerie! I thought Walkers were just a legend."

"They're real," I told her. "So you can see why we can't let the Cabal experiment on her or whatever the hell they're doing up there."

Christina nodded enthusiastically. "Yeah, of course. So how do we get her out?"

"We haven't decided that yet," Leon said.

She indicated the sack of Chinese food on the table. "So let's eat and figure it out."

"You sure you want to help us do this?" I asked. "You only came here for the changeling."

"Hell yeah I'm sure. I'm not going to turn down a chance to go toe-to-toe with the Midnight Cabal. This kind if stuff is the reason why I joined the Society all those years ago. When we were kids, my brother and I used to pretend that one of us was an evil wizard who had a princess locked away in a tower somewhere and the other was a knight hell-bent on rescuing her. We used climb over the furniture in our apartment, fighting with cardboard swords. That came to an end one day when he knocked our mother's favorite vase off a table and it smashed on the floor. After that, we were only allowed to play with the swords outside."

She got up and began the food from the paper sack. "Imagine my surprise some years later when I discovered the Society of Shadows was a real thing. There actually were knights in the world and I could become one of them."

"What about your brother?" Leon asked. "Did he join too?"

She stopped unpacking the food for a few seconds and looked down at the table with sadness in her eyes. "No, Tomás died when he was twelve years old from cancer. He never got the chance to save a princess." She resumed unpacking the food. "But that was a long time ago and since then, I discovered that the Society may not be so wonderful after all."

"Maybe not," I said, "Maybe the whole damn organization is corrupt but until it kicks me out, I'll use its resources and money to help people as much as I can."

"That's a good way of looking at it," she said, picking up a slice of pizza and taking a bite. "Now come and get some food while it's still hot."

Merlin arrived an hour later. He didn't drive his car to the cabin; instead, he appeared on foot as if taking an evening stroll. In his hand, he held Excalibur, wrapped in fabric. He was sauntering along the edge of the lake, oblivious to the heavy rain.

"Ah, Alec," he said when he saw me. "You forgot this." As he approached, he held the covered sword out to me.

"No thanks, I'm good," I said.

Shooting me a hard look, he rested the sword against the cabin wall near my chair. He was completely dry. The rain hadn't touched him. Who needs an umbrella when you can cast a spell to protect you from the elements?

"Where's your patrol car?" I asked.

"It's parked at the Lodge. That's where I've been staying."

I quirked an eyebrow. "Funny, I don't remember seeing it there after I told you to go back to Dearmont."

He smiled thinly. "That's because I didn't want you to see it. A simple spell took care of that." His eyes wandered to Christina and then back to me. "Aren't you going to introduce me to your new friend?"

"Christina, this is Sheriff John Cantrell," I said. I wasn't about to explain the whole Merlin thing. "John, this is Christina Flores, a P.I. From New York."

"A P.I. How delightful," he said, nodding to her. He spotted the leftovers on the table and went over to it. "Is anyone eating this? I'm ravenous."

"Help yourself," Christina said.

He began picking through the remains of the Chinese food and pizza. "So are we getting any closer to the Cabal?" This question was obviously directed at me even though his focus was on the food in front of him.

"Maybe," I said warily. If Merlin knew that we'd discovered a Cabal enclave, he'd be pushing Excalibur into my hand and insisting we go there immediately to kill everybody.

He sat down with a handful of eggrolls and said, "Tell me everything you know," before popping one of the rolls into his mouth.

Unwilling to do that, I said, "We don't know

much yet. I'll let you know when we have concrete information."

"And what am I supposed to do until then? Sit in my room and watch television?"

"Hey, I didn't ask you to come here."

"No, you didn't, and that makes me think you're not committed to fulfilling your end of the bargain you made with the Lady of the Lake."

Christina's eyes widened when she heard that. "Bargain? Is there something you haven't told me?"

Merlin turned his attention to her. "Allow me to bring you up to speed, Christina. I am Merlin. The sword wrapped in cloth over there is Excalibur. And Alec made an oath to the Lady of the Lake that he would bring down the Midnight Cabal."

She looked at me closely. "Is that true?"

"There's more to it than that but those are the basic facts, I guess."

"Wow, I thought I had an interesting career but you have me beat. Merlin? Excalibur? I feel like I just stepped into the middle of a fairy tale."

I gave her a non-committal smile but didn't say anything. I was pretty sure this tale wasn't going to have a happy ever after.

"So if you know anything about where the Cabal might be hiding," Merlin said as his eyes moved from me to Leon and then to Christina, "You need to reveal it to me now."

No one said anything.

He sighed and looked at me. "There's something you're not telling me. Am I going to have to use a spell to get it out of you?"

"Don't even think about it," I warned him.

He stood up. His fingers began moving in intricate patterns.

I also stood and as I did so, I felt anger rise within me. Along with that anger came an energy that spread through me until my entire body was suffused with it. A black magical circle materialized in my mind's eye. I'd seen this circle before, had used it at Rekhmire's lair to nullify a force field that had held Mallory and me hostage.

Merlin obviously didn't detect the magic rising within me. He went on casting his spell.

"I said no!" I said. As I spoke the words, a wave of black energy radiated from me. When it touched Merlin, it threw him off the porch. He tumbled through the air and splashed into the lake.

I tried to quell my anger as I felt the energy in my body subside.

Merlin climbed out of the lake. He wasn't dry anymore. Now he was drenched. But more satisfying than that was the fear I could see in his eyes.

I grabbed Excalibur and threw it into the dirt by his feet. "Get the hell out of here and take that fucking thing with you."

He didn't defy me, didn't say anything at all. He grabbed the cloth-covered sword and ran back toward the Lodge. As soon as he left the circle of light that spilled from the porch, the rain-filled night swallowed him.

Christina was staring at me with an expression of disbelief. "Dude, what the hell? Merlin the magician just got his ass handed to him. How did you do that?"

"It's just happens sometimes," I said. "I can't explain it."

She looked incredulous. "Well as unexplainable things go, that one is pretty big."

"Yeah." I sat down on the chair, already feeling weariness creep over me. I wasn't going to tell her about the etchings on my bones or the fact that the Coven had put them there with my father's blessing, or even under his direction. She'd come here to kill a changeling, not listen to the problems of my dysfunctional family.

"You okay, Alec?" Leon asked, concern on his face. He knew how much these magical episodes took out of me.

"I'll be fine," I said, even though I wasn't sure I would be. If I hadn't thrown Excalibur at Merlin, I could have touched the sword and received a hit of energy but now that wasn't an option. That was probably a good thing; I had to learn to handle these energy spikes and troughs without the help of anything or anyone else.

Christina, who by now must be wondering what the hell she'd gotten herself into, said, "Listen, I'm going to go and sort out a room at the Lodge. I'll see you guys in the morning." She got out of her chair and hurried through the rain to the Renegade.

She backed onto the dirt road and drove away, her headlights fading in the distance.

"Do you think she'll be back?" Leon said. "I'm sure she wasn't expecting all this when she came to kill that changeling."

"I don't think she's running away," I told him. "I think she's giving us some space. She probably needs to process just what the hell she's walked into the middle of but she seems tough. I'm sure she's going to see her job through and probably help us with the Cabal as well."

He nodded thoughtfully. "I hope so. Like you said, she seems tough. The kind of person we need on our side. Especially now we can't count on Merlin's help."

"Yeah, I may have screwed up that relationship but I couldn't let him cast a spell on us."

"No argument from me. I understand completely. I'd have blasted him off the porch too if I had the mojo."

"Believe me, this isn't something you want." My bones and muscles felt as if they were made of lead. My brain was foggy and sending the signal to my body that it needed to sleep and recover from the outpouring of energy that had just occurred.

"Yeah, I know how it affects you." He chuckled. "But blasting Merlin into the lake was a touch of genius. I wish I'd recorded it."

I laughed. "Yeah, it was kind of satisfying." The weariness was spreading through me and my eyelids were heavy. "We'll make our plans tomorrow. I'm going to hit the hay."

"Okay, man. See you in the morning."

I got up out of the chair and the world tipped beneath my feet. I leaned against the wall to steady myself.

"You need any help?" Leon asked.

"No, I just need a minute to get my balance." I took some deep breaths before going inside and climbing the stairs. When I got into my bedroom, I undressed quickly and collapsed onto the bed.

As soon as I closed my eyes, sleep wrapped me in its tight embrace and I dreamed of the Coven leaning over me and performing some sort of magical surgery on my body while my father looked on from the shadows.

When I awoke the following morning, I felt almost normal. A dull ache ran through my bones but other than that, I felt refreshed from the previous night's sleep, even if it had been full of dreams and half-remembered images dancing over my brain.

I slid out of bed and padded to the window. The morning was bright and the rain had ceased. The leaves of the trees glistened wetly as a reminder of the downpour but the sky was clear now and even though I knew the day would be cold, at least it would be dry.

I dressed and went downstairs where I found Leon and Christina sitting at the pine table in the living room eating pancakes.

"Hey, how are you?" Leon asked when he saw me.

"Good," I said. "I'll be even better if there are any pancakes left."

"It just so happens that there are plenty," he said, indicating a high stack sitting on a plate in the middle of the table. "And there's coffee too."

"Great," I said, taking a seat at the table. To Christina, I said, "So we didn't scare you away last night."

She smiled. "It takes more than an ancient wizard and black energy waves coming out of nowhere to scare this girl away."

"Glad to hear it."

"The only thing that worries me," she said, "is how the hell we're going to get into Butterfly Heights. That place is locked up tighter than Trump's tax returns."

"There's something else we need to consider too," I said. "If Cathy gets scared, she may open up a portal and escape through it. If that happens, we could lose her forever."

"So what's the plan?" she asked.

"We need to figure something out. I was going to call some friends so we'd have more firepower but if we go in with all guns blazing, we might scare Cathy away. A stealthy approach might be the best solution."

"That's going to be difficult," Leon said. "Remember those cameras we saw in every hallway? Even if we managed to get inside without being seen, there's no way we could avoid being seen by the cameras. Not unless you have an invisibility spell you'd like to share."

"I don't, unfortunately." I considered the problem. We couldn't use the hallways without tripping the building's security system and blasting our way in could spook Cathy and make her flee through a portal. We had to get to her room quietly and unseen.

"The mirrors," I said.

Christina looked at me with a puzzled expression but Leon knew what I was talking about. He nodded slowly. "The Shadow Land."

"Okay, don't tell me you guys have been to the Shadow Land," Christina said.

"We have," I told her.

She sighed and shook her head. "What the hell have I been doing with my life?" She speared a piece of pancake on her plate, used her fork to slide it through a pool of maple syrup she'd poured for just that purpose and placed it in her mouth thoughtfully.

"It could work," Leon said. "I remember seeing a large mirror in Cathy's bathroom."

"Mirrors?" Christina asked, chewing on another mouthful of pancake.

While I took a few pancakes of my own from the stack, Leon explained. "There's a way to travel to and from the Shadow Land using a spell and mirrors. We discovered that's how Mister

Scary moved about within the houses where he killed his victims."

"Mister Scary? Don't tell me you know him too."

"Maybe that's a story for another time," Leon said. "Anyway, there's a way to travel from one mirror to another. The only drawback is that you have to travel through the Shadow Land and that place is pretty dangerous."

"Even more so around Butterfly Heights," I said. "Shadow creatures tend to be attracted to people with mental health issues so in the shadow version of the Heights, there are going to be a few monsters."

"Monsters I can handle," Christina said. "If it means we have a way to get in there and save the girl, count me in."

I fished my phone out of my pocket and called Carlton. Felicity had been researching the mirror spell since we'd found out Mister Scary was using it and when she finally cracked the code, she recorded the spell in her notes. Knowing that Felicity's filing system was top-notch, I guessed that it shouldn't take Carlton long to locate the spell and send it to me.

He answered the phone with a cheery, "Hey, Alec, how's it going?"

"We're making progress," I told him. "I need you to find a spell that Felicity researched."

"No problem. What's it called?"

That gave me pause. If the spell had a proper name, I didn't know it. If Felicity had filed it under its proper name, it could be anywhere. "Um, I don't know. The mirror spell?"

"The mirror spell?" Carlton repeated, a hint of doubt in his voice. "That doesn't sound right. The correct naming convention for spells usually—"

"Yes, I know what the convention is." I tried to come up with likely possibilities. "The Evocation of—"

"Evocation? Does the spell summon beings from other realms?"

"No."

"Then it won't be an evocation."

"It's a transportation spell. It uses mirrors. And the Shadow Land. That's all I know."

There was a pause and then he said, "Hold on, I'm going to try something." I heard him put the phone down and open the filing cabinets in the office. After a few seconds he picked up the phone again. "Found it. The spell has a long Latin name but it basically translates to The Conveyance of the Body Through the Land of Shadow Using Reflections."

"You found that from my description?"

"No, I found it because Felicity filed it under Mirror Spell."

"Oh."

"She probably knew you'd call it that."

"Yeah." She knew me better than I thought. I

suddenly missed her so much it hurt. "I need you to get that spell to me."

"Sure thing. I'll copy it and email it over."

"Thanks, Carlton. How are things at the office?"

"Quiet. I'm taking the opportunity to catch up on some reading."

"Anything interesting?"

"Not really. Just hieroglyphs and whatnot. I feel like I could have been more useful on the Rekhmire case if I'd been more educated about this kind of thing."

"Carlton, you were fine."

"Yeah, maybe. But I've lost three P.I.s already. I don't want to lose you too, especially if something happened to you because of something I didn't know."

"Listen, brushing up on your hieroglyphs is great but don't beat yourself up over the past."

"I won't," he said but I was sure that was what was going on here. "I'll get that spell to you right away."

"Thanks, Carlton." I ended the call. "He'll send it over soon," I told Leon and Christina.

"And what's the plan once we have Cathy?" Christina asked. "We get her out of Butterfly Heights and away from the Cabal but what then?"

"The first thing we need to do is establish her trust," I said. "Then we need to convince her to open a portal to the same place she and her friend fled to that night in the woods. We need to go through and find Lydia. From the drawings Cathy made, it looks like she's also in the hands of the Cabal."

She nodded. "Another princess to save."

"Yeah," I said. "After that, I don't know. The fact is, Cathy's talent is so rare that I doubt the Cabal will ever stop chasing her."

Christina's face fell. "What a terrible life. To be pursued forever."

"We'll have to figure out a way to stop that from happening," I said. I wasn't overly confident, though. Now that the Cabal knew Cathy was a Walker of Worlds, they wouldn't let her slip through their fingers.

"We need to prepare our weapons for the journey through the Shadow Land," I said. "I suggest that as soon as the spell arrives, we use it and get Cathy out of there. The sooner the better."

Leon and Christina both nodded in agreement.

"Okay," I said. "Let's sharpen the swords and go to work."

21

"The tenth witch?" Felicity said. The fact that the Midnight Cabal had a witch as powerful as the nine she'd seen earlier in the otherworldly cavern made her afraid of what such an organization might do with that kind of power.

"Yes," Thomas said. He leaned against the lectern as if suddenly weak. "The Society of Shadows was formed by ten witches. From their realm, they watched over the world and tried to protect it from evil by sending Wardens to fight paranormal threats, wherever they arose. The Wardens—who later became the P.I.s—did a good job. Most of the world's inhabitants are unaware that preternatural creatures even exist."

The familiar sadness entered his eyes again. "But then the witches became aware of an organization that rivaled the Society in numbers and strength. The Midnight Cabal was believed to have been destroyed centuries earlier but it had endured, crawling beneath the skin of society. This was an enemy like no other. It had plans and resources and, worse than that, it had a philosophy. It believed that mankind should be plunged back into the dark ages of fear and ignorance."

"The Cabal was protected by powerful wards, its dealings mostly hidden from sight," he said. "The witches could not see what their enemies were doing, what they were planning. All attempts at magical surveillance were thwarted by the Cabal's protections. So the Coven came up with a plan. One of their number would come to the Earthly realm and work as a spy, discovering the Cabal's intentions and reporting back if the need arose."

He left the stage and sat wearily on the seat next to Felicity. "Choosing to become a spy and live on Earth as a normal human being was not a decision to be taken lightly. For one thing, leaving the realm where the Coven resides meant losing the immortality that realm offers. Whoever undertook the task would become mortal. But there was one witch willing to make that sacrifice. She left her sisters and became mortal, first living on Earth as a member of the Society while she remembered how to function as a human being again and then joining the Cabal."

"And now she's giving them prophecies," Felicity said. "Does that mean she's working for them rather than spying on them?"

He shook his head vehemently. "No, I can't believe that. She would never betray the Society. I fear the Cabal has discovered her true purpose for joining its ranks and is forcing her to provide the prophecies. She would never give them willingly."

"Are you sure about that?" Felicity asked. "The Cabal seems to be quite persuasive. Perhaps she decided to actually join the organization."

"Never," he said.

Felicity had no idea why he was so passionate about the witch's loyalty to the Society.

"Now, let's go and get the girl," he said, abruptly standing up. He strode to the rear of the lecture hall where the door was located. Felicity followed, choosing to say nothing. He was obviously having some sort of tantrum so she thought it best to let him get on with it. When he calmed down, she'd speak to him but until then she was going to keep quiet.

He pushed through the door and out into the hallway. He stopped and took a deep breath before saying, "I'm sorry. I just can't bear the thought that the Cabal has her captive. Or that she might have gone over to their side. I don't even know which is worse."

Leaning against the wall, he dropped his head and rubbed his eyes with the heel of his hand.

Felicity stayed a respectable distance away. She didn't know Thomas well enough to put her arm around his shoulder and try to comfort him.

"I'm just an old fool," he said, wiping his eyes and standing straight. He took in a deep breath and let it out quickly in an attempt to compose himself. "Just ignore me, Felicity."

"I don't want to ignore you," she told him. "I want to help if I can."

"There's nothing anyone can do," he said, "but thank you for the sentiment. Now, we must begin our mission. The timing of our infiltration into Butterfly Heights is crucial. We only have on shot at this." He began walking along the hallway.

"How are we going to get in?" Felicity asked.

"Through the front door," he said. "Right under their noses."

Excitement seemed to slowly overtake his earlier misery and he increased his pace. "We'll show them they're messing with the wrong people," he said. He pressed his hand against a door and led Felicity into a small room that housed an assortment of items from small statues to pieces of jewelry.

"These are the magical items at our disposal for now," he said. "Once the academy is up and running properly, we'll acquire many more, I'm sure. Right now, though, I think these will come in handy." He opened a closet in which two hooded cloaks hung from pegs.

"What are they?" Felicity asked.

"These cloaks were used by an order of assassins at various times in history. Watch this." He reached for one of the cloaks and put it on, fastening it at his neck with an emerald and gold clasp. Felicity expected some spell to be activated —an invisibility spell perhaps—but nothing happened.

"It isn't doing anything," she said.

"Not yet," he said, grinning. "But watch what happens when I pull the hood over my head. He reached back and pulled up the hood. His entire appearance, including his face, changed in an instant. Where gray-haired and bearded Thomas Harbinger had stood a moment ago clad in a tweed suit, there now stood a burly man with dark curly hair dressed in a dark sweater and jeans. The cloak was invisible.

"You're looking at Vasily Sokolov," the man said. The voice was unmistakably Thomas Harbinger's but it was coming from this entirely different man. "He's a Cabal operative. As long as I'm wearing the cloak with the hood over my head, I will appear to be him."

He indicated the other cloak with a wave of his hand. "Try that one on. The cloaks can be made to look like anyone. These have been prepared to mimic two Cabal agents. So now you can see how we're going to walk in through the front door, eh?"

"I suppose so," Felicity said, picking up the other cloak and putting it on. "But is an altered appearance going to be enough to get us inside? What if they demand to see our ID or something?"

The man who looked like Vasily Sokolov reached up and seemed to brush back the hair on both sides of his face. As his hands reached the back of his head, he became Thomas Harbinger again, pushing back the hood.

"We're prepared for that eventuality," he said, picking up two small cards from a table. He handed one to Felicity and she inspected it. Painted on both of the cards black surfaces were a red unicursal hexagram and other esoteric symbols.

"What's this?" she asked.

"If someone asks for my ID and I show them this card, that's what they'll see."

"Vasily Sokolov's ID?"

He nodded. "Now put your hood up and we'll see how you look in your new identity."

Felicity pulled the hood over her head. She didn't feel any different and when she looked down at herself, she saw her own clothes and body. "I don't think it worked."

He chuckled. "The magic works on people looking at you but it doesn't fool you. Here, take a look in this mirror." He angled an ornate full-length mirror so that it reflected Felicity. When she saw herself, she took a step back in surprise. Her reflection was that of a Vietnamese woman in her thirties wearing a white lab coat.

"Doctor Irene Tran," Thomas said. "She's a scientist who's quite high up the Cabal ranks. You'll have no trouble getting into Butterfly Heights looking like her."

"I look like her," Felicity said, unable to tear her eyes away from her altered reflection in the mirror, "but I don't sound like her."

"No, you don't. And I don't sound like Vasily either. The assassins who used these cloaks would practice for weeks mimicking their targets. Unfortunately we don't have time for that so we're just going to have to wing it."

Felicity pushed the hood from her head. Her reflection immediately changed back to normal. "We won't be able to get inside without speaking."

"True but I doubt anyone at Butterfly Heights has ever met Vasily or Irene so we should be okay. And how many people are we going to have to speak to anyway? Probably only the receptionist and he or she won't know the difference between us and the real Cabal members." He held up the card with the esoteric symbols. "And we have ID to back up who we say we are."

Felicity didn't share his optimism. Using these disguises to get into Butterfly Heights seemed risky. "Assuming we get to the girl, what then?"

He reached into his pocket and held up an ornate item that looked like a Fabergé egg. He'd used one of these to open a portal to this realm from the Earthly realm. "I'll activate this, we step through the portal, and we all end up back at the academy."

"So why don't we just portal in and out? It sounds much safer."

"We can't portal in there," he said, "because I don't know where Cathy is located within the building. If we suddenly appear in the corridor or in someone else's room, we'll never be able to explain what we're doing there."

"Oh," she said.

"I can portal us to the outside of the building, though," he offered. "At least we won't have far to walk."

"Will we be taking weapons in case anything goes wrong?" She didn't like the idea of having to fight her way out of a Cabal stronghold but she'd feel better if she was armed.

"Of course. We should have time to visit the armory and then be on our way."

"Are we in a hurry?"

"We have to time our appearance at Butterfly Heights exactly with Alec's."

"Alec? Will he be there?" Felicity suddenly felt

more optimistic. If Alec was going to be at Butterfly Heights, the chances of survival just increased exponentially.

"Yes, he'll be there," Thomas said, opening the door and ushering her out of the room. "At least he will if we time this right." He checked his watch as they strode along the hallway. "Time passes differently in this realm so I have to make a few mental calculations. We have to get to Cathy's room at the same time as Alec. We can't get there before him because these flimsy disguises don't really afford us the luxury of waiting around. If we arrive after him, we might miss the portal."

"Portal?"

He nodded. "There's a chance that when Alec arrives, Cathy will activate a portal. If she does, we have to be there when that happens."

"Why?"

"Because we're supposed to go through it."

"I thought you were going to use your egg to get us back here."

"Yes, that's one possibility. That's what will happen if Cathy doesn't open a portal of her own."

"And if she does, we're supposed to go through it?"

"That's right." He pressed a door that opened into a room whose walls were hung with swords, daggers, staffs, and bows.

"What happens after we go through the portal?"

He grimaced. "Even the witches don't know about that. The future becomes very fluid at that point." He gestured to the weapons on the wall. "Grab one of these and let's get going."

22

Leon, Christina, and I arrived at the Butterfly Heights parking lot in my Land Rover. We'd hardly spoken during the drive over here. I'd been thinking about what lay ahead and what might go wrong. I didn't want to dwell on the negatives of our plan but I wanted to be prepared for any eventuality.

As far as I could tell, the biggest risk was that Cathy would panic, open a portal, and escape through it. That was the worst-case scenario because if she closed the portal behind her, we'd have no way of reaching her or even knowing where she'd gone. She'd be lost in another realm, probably one where the Cabal had agents or soldiers on the lookout for her. It would probably only be a matter of time before they recaptured her.

Before we got to her room, though, we had to

make it through the Shadow Land. Leon and I had been there before and come through relatively unscathed and Mallory had survived there for months but I would never treat that place with anything but the fearful respect it deserved. Taking a place like the Shadow Land for granted could lead to instant death.

That was why we'd decided to enter the Shadow Land in the woods near Butterfly Heights. That way, we wouldn't have to travel too far before we reached the mirror in Cathy's room and stepped back into this realm. The less time we spent in the shadows, the better.

I opened the trunk and between us, Leon and I carefully lifted out the full-length mirror we'd brought from the bedroom at *Pine Retreat*. Christina grabbed a black Adidas gym bag, into which we'd stowed our weapons, and we set off into the woods.

I'd already cast the spell to charge the mirror, reading the words from an email Carlton had sent. All we had to do now was place our bloody palms on the glass and step through into the realm of nightmares.

Manhandling the large mirror up the steep path wasn't easy but we managed to get to a spot close enough that we could see Butterfly Heights but still be concealed by the trees. We left the path and set up the mirror in a place where no one else would see it, leaning against the thick trunk of an old pine tree.

Christina opened the gym bag and distributed the weapons. We each had a sword and a dagger. That would be enough to see us through most situations but not so much that we were weighed down with weaponry. We might have to move fast so traveling light was the best option.

"I'll go first," I said, using my dagger to cut a small diagonal line in my palm. I placed it against the mirror's glass and instantly felt the surface shift beneath my touch. I pushed my hand forward and it went through the glass. Not knowing what was on the other side—there could be a monster waiting there to bite my arm off for all I knew—I quickly stepped through the mirror and found myself in the shadow version of the woods.

The shadow woods were dark and I waited for my eyes to adjust to the gloom. The enchanted sword in my hand cast a sickly blue glow that was too weak to illuminate my surroundings.

Christina stepped through the shadow version of the mirror and looked around, her eyes wide. "This place lives up to its name."

"Your eyes should adjust in a minute," I said.

She cocked her head to one side. "Is my hearing adjusting too or did I just hear something slithering through the trees over there?" She pointed to our right.

I listened but then Leon came through the mirror and said, "Man, this place never changes."

I held up a hand and he went quiet.

"We may not be alone," I whispered.

He nodded in understanding and looked around at the shadowy trees.

"You hear that?" Christina whispered.

This time I did hear it; a low rustle like a snake slithering through wet leaves. I nodded and pointed in the direction the sound was coming from. "There's something over there."

"So let's go this way," Leon whispered, pointing at the shadow version of Butterfly Heights. "The sooner we get to the mirror in Cathy's room, the better."

I couldn't argue with that. I didn't want to be in this place for one second more than I had to be. I gingerly stepped in the direction of the building, trying to make as little noise as possible.

I'd barely taken three steps when the ground around us erupted and the body of a giant snake emerged from the dead leaves. We were standing inside a coil of scales. The head, which was what we'd heard to our right, reared up from the trees.

It was no ordinary snake. It wasn't even an ordinary giant snake. Long octopus-like tentacles writhed where its head should be and two milky yellow orbs that must have served as eyes gazed down at us.

"Everybody move!" I shouted. "It's going to strike!"

We scattered as the head shot forward and the tentacles speared the ground where we'd been standing.

I was close to the coiled body now; the scales shifting as the muscles beneath them pulsated and the snake slithered forward.

I raised my sword above my head with both hands and brought it down swiftly, hoping to sever the body. The blade bounced harmlessly off the scales. They were as strong as steel.

Something touched around my ankle and I looked down in time to see a tentacle insidiously weaving around my leg. Instinctively, I stabbed at it with the sword and it retreated.

Leon and Christina were also attacking the body and discovering the strength of the creature's scales.

"How do we kill it?" Christina shouted.

"Go for the eyes." They seemed to be the creature's only weak spot but the head was currently about twenty feet in the air, out of reach of our weapons.

"We should have brought a bow," Leon said.

"When it strikes again," I said. "The eyes will be closer. Too far away for a sword strike but maybe we can throw the daggers."

We grouped together and waited, each of us holding a dagger by the blade's tip.

The creature's head reared up again and then shot at us, tentacles writhing.

I rolled into a crouch and threw my dagger. It spun through the air and buried itself deep in the creature's eyes, which burst open like a lanced boil and spewed yellow fluid.

A sharp-toothed maw opened between the base of the tentacles and widened as if screaming but no sound emerged from the creature's throat. The other eye had also exploded. Either Christina or Leon's daggers, or maybe both of them, had struck home.

The scaly body began flicking and coiling crazily, smashing into trees and slamming against the ground.

"We need to get out of here!" I shouted. "Now!"

We sprinted past the flailing body, ducking and weaving to avoid the writhing tip of the snake-thing's tail, which was armed with a barb as big as a spear. Leon rolled out of its way as it embedded itself into the trunk of a tree. As we left the area and I looked back over my shoulder, I saw that the tree had withered and died instantaneously, probably from a massive dose of deadly poison.

"What the hell was that thing?" Christina asked breathlessly.

"Something that only exists in this crazy place," Leon said.

We made our way to Butterfly Heights. The shadow version of the building looked exactly like its real-world counterpart except for a few areas that seemed insubstantial and made of black smoke. Luckily for us, part of the outer wall was missing. We walked through the smoke and onto the lawn.

Shadowy figures ambled about the place. Their heads were lowered, their gait barely more than a shuffle.

"Are these the patients?" Christina asked.

"The shadow versions of them," I said. "Some of them may not even be residents here anymore but their thoughts have left behind shadow versions of themselves."

She looked at the shuffling shadows and shook her head. "So sad."

We approached the building and found parts of the wall were missing here too so we stepped through into the reception area. More figures shuffled around in here. They seemed totally aimless as they wandered around the room.

We made our way through the corridors, passing through doors that were locked in our reality but were no more than shadowy smoke here. When we reached Cathy Pelletier's room, I went through the door first and saw a shadow version of Cathy sitting on the sofa watching TV.

I made my way to the bathroom and waited for the others.

Leon and Christina joined me and I pointed at the shadow version of the large bathroom mirror. "That's our way into the room. When we go through, we need to make sure we don't startle Cathy."

"Dude, we're going to walk out of her bathroom mirror," Leon said. "She's going to be startled."

"I know. But maybe she won't open a portal if we can calm her down."

He shrugged. "It's worth a try. But what if she does open a portal?"

"If she flees, we go after her. There's a good chance that any portal she opens will be to the same place she went last time, so she might lead us to Lydia."

"Two birds with one stone," Christina said.

I nodded and spoke the words of the Conveyance of the Body Through the Land of Shadow Using Reflections—aka the Mirror Spell —to charge the mirror. When that was done, I used the tip of my sword to cut my hand and placed it on the shadowy substance that represented glass in this realm.

Then I stepped through.

23

"Are you ready?" Thomas asked.

Felicity nodded. She was as ready as she was ever going to be. She was wearing the assassin's cloak and she had a sword attached to her belt. If the stealth afforded by the cloak failed, the sword would hopefully help her get out of danger.

He placed one of the egg devices on the floor of the armory and the air shimmered before tearing open to show woodland beyond.

"They don't stay open for long," Thomas said. "We need to move quickly." He stepped through the portal and Felicity followed. A second later, she was standing in the woods and the portal was closing behind her.

"We'd best put our disguises on now," Thomas said, pulling up his hood and transforming into Vasily Sokolov.

Felicity did the same and asked, "How do I look?"

"Perfect," he said. "We shouldn't have any trouble getting inside."

They made their way through the trees, searching for the path that would take them to Butterfly Heights. Felicity knew that as long as they were ascending the hill, they were going in the right direction. But they had to be on the path by the time they reached the building in case any security cameras were watching. It might seem strange if Vasily Sokolov and Dr Iren Tran suddenly appeared out of the woods.

She saw something glinting in the dull sunlight and moved toward it.

"What is it?" Thomas asked.

"It looks like a mirror." As she got closer, she saw three bloody handprints on the glass and realized what the mirror had been used for. "The Conveyance of the Body Through the Land of Shadow Using Reflections," she said.

Thomas frowned. "What's that?"

"A spell for getting to the Shadow Land. Three people have used it and passed through this mirror."

"It must be Alec," he said.

"Yes," she said, smiling. "It must be."

"Don't worry, you'll see him soon enough," Thomas said. He checked his watch. "But we must get inside as soon as possible."

After a couple of minutes, they found the path and followed it to the high wrought iron gate that led to the lawn.

Thomas pressed the intercom and waited. He looked confident, as if he really was a Cabal agent and he belonged here.

When the intercom crackled and a male voice asked, "Can I help you?" Thomas put on a Russian accent. "I am Vasily Sokolov here to visit with one of your patients."

There was a pause and then the voice said, "Do you have an appointment?"

Thomas sighed and said, "Young man, I do not need an appointment. I am Vasily Sokolov."

"I'm afraid you do need an appointment, Mr Sokolov. If you'd like—"

"I'd like to come inside," Thomas said. "Check my name on your computer and you will see that you should allow me access to your facility if you wish to keep your job. Do you wish to keep your job?"

There was a longer pause and then the voice said, "Come in." The gate buzzed and swung open.

Thomas strode across the lawn confidently and Felicity kept pace with him, reminding herself that she was Dr Irene Tran and she had every right to be here.

The door to the reception area was open when they reached it and they entered the building. Sitting behind the reception desk was a fair-haired young man in his early twenties and on his computer screen was a photograph of Vasily Sokolov. The receptionist had obviously looked up Sokolov in the Cabal database and realized that the threats uttered over the intercom were not idle.

"Mr Sokolov," he said, "Welcome to Butterfly Heights." His gaze shifted to Felicity. "And you are?"

"This is Dr Tran," Thomas said. "She is with me. We wish to visit with Cathy Pelletier, if you please."

The young man pursed his lips and hesitated.

"Our time is valuable," Thomas reminded him.

"Perhaps I should see some identification," the receptionist said. "It's the rules."

"I understand. In Russia, we follow rules." Thomas produced the card with the esoteric symbols upon its faces and passed it to the young man, saying, "This is my ID."

Felicity brought out her own card and held it up. "This is my ID." She wondered if the verbal clues helped to sell the illusion.

The young man squinted at her card and nodded. He was clearly seeing something other than a unicursal hexagram. "Everything seems to be in order," he said. "I'll just get a keycard printed for you." He fiddled with a machine beneath his desk for a few seconds and then handed a plastic card to Thomas. "There's a simple map on the back of the card but it's just through that door and then follow the corridor to the left. It's door number 6."

"Thank you," Thomas said. He and Felicity walked to the door that led to the inner part of the building and opened it with the card. They turned left and followed the corridor.

Felicity was aware of the cameras on the walls and kept her head down despite the disguise she wore. Neither she nor Thomas spoke.

When they reached the door they were looking for, Thomas checked his watch. "Remember," he said, "You can tell Alec about the academy but not its purpose. He must not be made aware of the end-times prophecy in any way."

"I understand," she said, even though she didn't.

He continued staring at his watch. "Just a few seconds more. If she opens a portal, be ready to move quickly."

Felicity nodded.

"Right," he said. "It's time." He reached forward and opened the door.

24

I stepped into Cathy's room and held up my hands in a placating gesture when her eyes widened and her body tensed.

At that same moment, the door to the room opened and two people entered; a burly dark-haired man and a woman in a white lab coat.

Behind me, I was aware of Leon and Christina coming through the bathroom mirror.

"It's all right, Cathy," the dark-haired man said. "We're here to help you."

Although I didn't know this man, his voice sounded eerily like my father's.

Cathy shrank back on the bed and I realized the stupidity of my plan to come through her bathroom mirror and not have her panic. Of course she was going to panic. The only question was how much would she panic. I hoped she didn't open a portal right now because even though I wanted to find Lydia, I didn't want to go leaping into the unknown at this moment.

I wanted time to plan and to gather reinforcements before entering a part of Faerie that was controlled by the Cabal.

That was a luxury I wouldn't be afforded. The air above the bed crackled and a bright lightning-like rent appeared in the air. Cathy's eyes became bright violet. The crack in the air widened and I could see a green meadow beyond. Cathy scrambled through the portal.

I wasted no time in following her. I bounded onto the bed and through the glowing rip in the barrier between realms, landing on my feet in the meadow. Cathy was running for the far end of the meadow, where a stream ran along the edge of a forest. A hill rose from the trees and a castle perched on the hill. This was the place in Cathy's drawing. This was where the Cabal had captured Lydia Cornell.

Christina jumped through the portal, followed closely by Leon. Then the two strangers came through. I drew my sword and held it tightly. "Who the hell are you?"

"Alec," the woman said, moving forward and raising her hands to her hair. Her appearance changed suddenly and she now looked like Felicity. "It's me," she said. "These are disguises we used to get into Butterfly Heights."

The man performed the same gesture with his

hands and now it was my father standing there. "Son," he said with a smile. "It's good to see you again."

I didn't feel the same way. I had too many questions that needed to be answered before I could decide what my feelings were regarding my father.

"What are you guys doing here?" Leon asked.

"We came to rescue Cathy," my dad said. "We know she's a Walker and we can't let the Cabal have her."

"Er, guys," Christina said. "The Walker is currently a runner and she's running into the forest."

"Yeah, we'll talk later," I said. "Right now, we need to get Cathy. I'm pretty sure that castle is a Cabal stronghold." I sprinted toward the forest. Everyone else followed.

Cathy reached the stream and stopped in her tracks. Maybe it was too deep for her to get across. She looked back at us with a look of pure fear in her eyes and then at the stream. Now that I was closer, I could see that it was fast running and probably deep. That wasn't the norm for the idyllic land of Faerie but maybe the Cabal's presence here had tainted the place.

I stopped running and motioned for the others to do the same. "Cathy," I said, "I promise we're not here to hurt you. We want to help find Lydia. She's here, isn't she? In that castle?"

She looked briefly at the castle on the hill then back at me, fear still burning in her eyes. If not for the stream, she'd be deep in the forest by now.

I walked slowly toward her, my hands open and raised. "Please don't run. We can help you."

"They did bad things to me," she said. "They put needles in my arms and took my blood. Every day. Over and over."

"I'm sorry about that," I said. "I truly am. But we aren't those people. We want to help you, not hurt you."

She shook her head. "I don't believe you."

"Listen," I said. "We won't come any closer. You can step away from the water's edge."

"You were with my aunt," she said. "She's a monster and you were with her."

"I didn't know what she was. Now that I know, I won't let her near you again. I protect people from monsters."

"It's true, Cathy," Christina said, stepping forward. "Alec protects people and so do I. We're here to protect you if you'll let us."

Cathy hesitated, turning her face to the turbulent water at her feet.

"Look at me, Cathy," Christina said. "It's time to stop running. When I was around your age, my brother died and I ran away from everything in my life. I was just so angry, you know? But I couldn't run away from the fact that Tomás was dead. That pain followed me everywhere I went.

It still follows me to this day. But I learned that I had to accept it."

She moved a little closer to Cathy. "You're a very special person, and I think you're trying to run away from that. Maybe that's why you wouldn't talk to anyone after you found out what you can do. You tried to hide inside yourself. But it's okay to be special. Sure, there are some problems that come with that but who doesn't have problems?"

Cathy took a deep breath and then she said to Christina, "Did your brother really die?"

Christina nodded sadly. "He did."

"My dad died. And I think my friend Lydia is in big trouble." Tears sprang into her eyes and she tried to wipe them away but they kept coming. "I didn't mean for it to happen. They took her up there and locked her away." She pointed at the castle, her chest hitching as she tried to hold back more tears.

Christina went to the girl and put her arms around her. Cathy broke down, slumping against Christina's shoulder and weeping.

I turned to the others. "We need to get Lydia back."

"Agreed," Leon said.

My father nodded. "I agree but we may be slightly outnumbered."

The air around became charged as if an electrical storm was about to discharge a bolt of lightning. A purple line appeared in the air, reaching to the ground before opening enough to let Merlin step through. The portal closed behind him and disappeared.

"What are you doing here?" I said.

"You know exactly what I'm doing here, Alec. I am here to ensure that you fulfill your pledge to the Lady of the Lake."

"How did you find me?"

He smiled thinly. "I can't track you because of those tattoos on your body but I can track him." He pointed at Leon. "And Faerie is my old stomping ground. I'm familiar with every inch of these meadows. Although some things seem to have changed. That castle wasn't there before."

In his hands, he held Excalibur, still wrapped in cloth. He held the bundle out to me with both hands. "Take it," he said. "Fulfill your destiny."

I looked at the wrapped sword. This was a weapon that would allow me to rescue Lydia Cornell from the Cabal. Could I refuse to help an innocent girl who had arrived here by accident and been taken prisoner?

I turned to Leon, Felicity, and my father. "Does anyone have any other ideas?"

"I'm afraid not," my father said. "We could try to storm the castle with our usual weapons but unfortunately, I don't think we'd get very far."

I turned back to Merlin. "If I do this, my

pledge is fulfilled. You go back to where you came from and take the sword with you."

"Just take it," he said, pushing the sword toward me.

"I'm only going to get Lydia out," I said, mostly to myself. "I'll take down anyone who gets in my way but once I find Lydia, I'm not sticking around to kill more Cabal members just because the Lady of the Lake wants me to."

I took the sword from Merlin's hands and unwrapped it. I felt its power coursing up my arm and through my body. I turned toward the castle.

Everything I'd just said was forgotten

I wanted to kill.

I needed to kill.

25

The walk through the woods to the foot of the hill seemed to take mere seconds. I felt as if I were floating, my feet inches above the ground. Felicity, my father, and Leon struggled to keep up with me. Christina had stayed at the stream with Cathy. What was about to happen was not something a young girl should witness.

A flagstone path led up the hill. As I ascended quickly, the others lagged behind, calling to me to wait for them. I couldn't wait. I had a job to do.

The first Cabal members I encountered met me at the castle gate. The looks on their faces told me they thought I was crazy to take them on alone. After all, I was one man and they numbered fifteen. What happened next was a blur of flashing swords, shouts of pain, and bloody corpses. The fifteen lay dead while the one remained standing.

I stalked into the castle where yet more members of the Cabal were gathered. They looked surprised to see me. They probably wondered how I'd gotten past the fifteen guards at the gate. I showed them.

When I was done, at least two dozen people lay in the courtyard. Excalibur throbbed in my hand. I felt invincible. There were shouts and the sound of booted feet running toward me. I wanted them to come. All of them. The more that came, the more would fall beneath my blade and the more energy the sword would drink from their dying bodies.

When they reached me, I whirled, slashed, thrust, and parried. The air was thick with the sound of steel and the smell of blood. There were so many bodies that I had to step on them to meet the new foes that came pouring out into the courtyard.

I laughed as my enemies fell. Excalibur felt like a living thing in my hand, its heartbeat aligned with my own.

Together we attacked, parried, jabbed, cut.

We fought together until the enemies stopped coming and I stood alone in the courtyard. My body was slick with blood. None of it was my own.

~

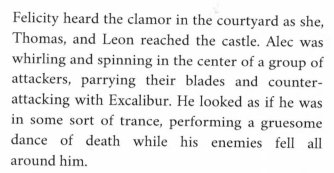

Felicity heard the clamor in the courtyard as she, Thomas, and Leon reached the castle. Alec was whirling and spinning in the center of a group of attackers, parrying their blades and counter-attacking with Excalibur. He looked as if he was in some sort of trance, performing a gruesome dance of death while his enemies fell all around him.

This isn't him, she told herself. *The sword is making him do this.* Even though the scene in the courtyard was a grisly one of blood and death, she found it difficult to tear her eyes away.

Leon put a hand on her shoulder. "We need to find Lydia."

"Yes, of course." She indicated a closed wooden door. "Let's see where this leads."

"Allow me," Thomas said, taking the lead. With his sword gripped in one hand, he used the other to open the door and then rushed inside, weapon ready. Felicity followed, with Leon guarding the rear.

They stood in a long, arch-ceilinged hallway. Flaming torches hung on the walls, casting an orange glow over the stone walls.

"Is medieval in this year?" Leon asked.

"We're in Faerie," Thomas said. "Modern

electrical lights don't work here. Nor do modern weapons. Not reliably, anyway. That's good for us because if the people out there had machine guns, we'd all be dead by now."

"If this castle is laid out in the traditional manner," Felicity said, "Then it's likely that there are dungeons underground. That's probably where they're holding Lydia."

"If she's still alive at all," Thomas said grimly. "The Midnight Cabal won't spare her just because she's a child."

"She's still alive," Felicity said firmly, not sure if she was trying to convince Thomas or herself. "We just have to find her."

He nodded. "Then we'll have to look for a way to get down to the dungeons."

They progressed along the corridor, weapons ready in case they should meet any opposition but all of the Cabal members seemed to be out in the courtyard. Felicity silently prayed that Alec could handle all of them. He seemed to be doing okay at the moment but she knew the sword was giving him power and could just as easily take that power away.

She was irked that Merlin, who'd given Alec the sword and sent him to the castle, was not getting involved in the fight himself. When they'd started up the hill, the wizard had stayed behind.

This was the time they needed him most of all. In the past, he seemed to be trying to become part of the their group but now she detected some kind of animosity between him and Alec. Had something happened between the two of them since she'd left Dearmont?

They reached a set of stone steps that led up to the next level. There was a lot of noise up there. The clatter of weapons, the sound of boots on flagstones. "Quickly," she said to the others. "We need to find a way down."

They increased their pace. From somewhere in the castle, commands were being shouted, weapons being drawn.

"Here," Thomas said, pointing at a set of stone steps ahead that descended into the hill.

They reached the top of the steps. The steep descent was lit with torches and the smell of damp wafted up from below.

"Someone's coming," Felicity said when she heard the clatter of metal and the rapid beat of boot leather on the steps.

Thomas sprang into action, rushing down to meet the enemy, the blue glow of his sword illuminating a hard expression in his eyes. Felicity and Leon followed quickly.

Three men and two women appeared below, dressed in dull plate armor. They didn't wear helmets and Felicity saw the surprise in their eyes as they saw the three strangers above them on the steps.

Taking advantage of the element of surprise,

Thomas leapt forward, swinging his sword hard and fast, hitting his opponents with the flat of the blade. It clanged against the plate armor of two of the men, the blow forceful enough to knock them off their feet. They fell back into their comrades and all five tumbled down the steps, weighed down by their armor.

Felicity descended quickly, telling herself that what she was about to do was necessary. These people were trying to destroy the world. Somewhere below, an innocent girl was being held captive.

The first Cabal member she reached was one of the men. He'd dropped his own weapon during the tumble down the stairs and he held up a gauntleted hand to try and stop what he must have known was coming.

Felicity saw fear in his eyes and hesitated for a split second. But she reminded herself again that the Cabal wanted to enslave the human race to fear and she thrust the tip of her sword between the plates of the man's armor and into his chest. The enchanted blade continued through the body until its tip met the plates that armored the man's back.

At least it's quick, she told herself as she withdrew the blade and continued down the steps to the next Cabal member, a woman who was getting to her feet and brandishing a sword.

When she saw Felicity and her fallen

comrades—Thomas and Leon had already killed two of the other Cabal members and Thomas was fighting the last man standing—the woman roared in anger and swung her sword wildly at Felicity's head.

Felicity parried the weapon and the sound of steel on enchanted steel rang from the blades.

Knowing she had to counterattack before this woman overwhelmed her with sheer brutality, Felicity thrust the tip of her sword at her enemy's face. The attack was blocked with a flick of the woman's sword and Felicity's blade clanged against the wall.

She had to act quickly as the woman performed a thrust as if she were a professional fencer. Felicity swept her blade downward, knocking the deadly attack aside, before slashing at the woman's face again.

This time, the enchanted blade cut through flesh and the woman—instinctively trying to raise her arms to protect herself—left herself open to further attacks.

Changing the angle of her blade, Felicity performed a fencing thrust much as the woman had just done, the difference being that Felicity's blade hit home. Its tip jabbed into the plate armor and cut through it like butter, going all the way through the woman's body.

With a look of surprise on her face, the Cabal member grabbed the blade of the enchanted weapon as if she could pull it out of herself but then her hands dropped to her sides and her body went limp. The sudden dead weight on her sword threatened to drag Felicity downward. She pulled the blade and quickly withdrew it as the dead body clattered down the steps.

If any other Cabal members were down there, they'd know someone was coming and they'd be ready. Felicity quickly descended the rest of the steps. She was sure Cathy's friend was down here somewhere and she was desperate to find her. She could hear Thomas and Leon behind her, trying to keep up.

At the bottom of the steps, an archway led to a long hallway lined with thick wooden doors that Felicity assumed were the doors of cells. Each door had a hatch at eye level and at the moment, all of the hatches were closed. Each door was secured with three heavy metal bolts.

"She's somewhere here," Felicity said, going to the first hatch and opening it. When she peered through, the saw a room with a high, barred window. A simple cot had been placed beneath the window and there was a crude wooden board with it a hole cut in it that served as a toilet but other than that, the room was unfurnished.

Felicity felt her heart sink. If that poor girl was being held in these barbaric conditions, she must have suffered mentally even if the Cabal hadn't done anything to harm her physically.

She rushed along the row of doors, opening the hatches and checking the cells while Leon and Thomas did the same on the other side of the hallway.

When Felicity opened a hatch and saw a dark-haired girl sitting on the cot in one of the cells, she said, "Lydia!"

The girl looked up at her. Her brown eyes looked haunted.

"I'm coming in," Felicity said, drawing back the bolts on the door. When she'd unlocked the cell, she pulled the door open and stepped inside.

Lydia shrank back.

"I'm here to rescue you," Felicity said softly. "Would you like to go home?"

The girl nodded.

Felicity held out her hand. She only half-expected the girl to take it but Lydia reached out and wrapped her fingers around Felicity's palm. Tears had begun to well in her eyes.

"You're safe now," Felicity assured her. "We're getting out of here. Your friend Cathy can't wait to see you again."

"Is she here?" Lydia asked.

"Yes, she is."

The barest flicker of a smile played over Lydia's face. "She came back for me. I knew she would. She didn't mean for this to happen."

"No, she didn't. Now, let's get out of here so

you can see her again and then we'll get you home."

"My mom will be worried," Lydia said.

"Yes, she will. Come on."

The girl allowed Felicity to lead her out into the hallway. Expecting to find Leon and Thomas there, Felicity was surprised to see neither of them. One of the cells at the far end of the hallway was open and voices were coming from within.

"Wait here," she told Lydia. "I just need to check on my friends."

Lydia shook her head and grasped Felicity's hand tighter. "Please don't leave me," she whispered. "I want to come with you."

Felicity assessed the risk. The sounds coming from the cell were not the sounds of a fight or an argument but the soft voices of people speaking. Gingerly, she led Lydia to the open cell door and peered inside.

Leon was standing by the wall, looking down at Thomas who was kneeling on the floor. Cradled in Thomas's arms was a dark-haired woman who looked to be in her sixties. She looked weak, as if she'd been drained of her life force.

She was dressed in jeans and a black sweater but there was something odd about her attire. Felicity looked closer. Black steel manacles inscribed with white magical symbols were fixed around the woman's ankles, wrists, and neck.

Thomas realized Felicity was there and looked up at her. His eyes and cheeks were shiny with tears. "This is the tenth witch," he said. "The one I told you about. The Cabal forced the prophecies from her, just as I said. She never betrayed us."

The woman turned her face toward the door and Felicity realized with a jolt that she'd seen her before. It had been only briefly, while escaping the Greek island of Dia after rescuing Gloria from the Cabal's clutches. This woman had been there, leading a regiment of Cabal soldiers.

With a sudden realization, Felicity said, "You're—"

"Yes," the woman said. "Now could either you or Leon please go and fetch Alec? I need to see my son."

26

I stood in the courtyard, breathing hard. The smell of death hung in the air like a heavy pall. Fallen Cabal members lay all around me and the clamor of noise that had been the constant accompaniment to the fighting was gone, Silence reigned.

The overpowering energy that the sword had transferred to me after each kill still swam in my blood and lit up every nerve ending in my body.

"*Alec,*" a voice said, slipping into my mind. "*Accept me fully and together we will destroy worlds and raise kingdoms.*"

I looked at the sword in my hand. Its blade shone and hummed with power.

I tore my gaze away from the light glinting along the blade in an almost hypnotic rhythm. The sword had come alive after killing so many people and now it had a heartbeat. My eyes fixed on the carnage all around us. When I'd entered the castle, my feelings had been overwhelmed by a bloodlust that had infused every atom of my being but now even that was fading as a sense of numbness gradually seeped over me.

"*Look at me,*" the sword urged, its voice sliding insidiously into my thoughts.

I ignored it.

"*We did this together. We vanquished our enemies. Together, we can do more. So much more.*"

For a moment, I was tempted to take it up on its offer. With the sword's help, I'd managed to destroy most of this castle's occupants in one swift blow. But this place was only an outpost. I imagined the damage I could do if I took Excalibur into one of the main Cabal buildings. I could wipe out the entire organization.

"*Yes,*" Excalibur whispered into my mind. "*We can kill them all.*"

A sudden revulsion washed over me and I threw the sword aside. I'd come here to rescue an imprisoned girl, not to go on a killing spree. It was Excalibur that had wrought this destruction; I'd merely been the hand holding its hilt, a puppet controlled by the puppet master.

The sickly smell in the air suddenly made me feel ill. I reeled away from the death that surrounded me and made it to the castle gate before I dropped to my knees and puked. As I spat the last of the bitter vomit onto the ground, I heard Leon's voice behind me.

"Alec, you need to come down to the dungeon."

"Sounds like an offer I can't refuse," I said, staggering to my feet and turning around. Leon stood there with Felicity and a young dark-haired girl who was clutching Felicity's hand.

"This is Lydia," Felicity said. "I'm going to get her out of here."

I nodded. "Good idea."

"Alec," Leon said, turning to a door. "There's someone you need to see."

"Okay," I said, following him. "Who is it?"

"It's best if you see for yourself. I don't think she has much time. We need to hurry." He increased his pace and I did likewise. My curiosity was piqued but I had no idea who he was taking me to see.

We descended a set of stairs that was littered with bodies and arrived in what was obviously the dungeon. The Cabal didn't have much imagination when it came to interior design; this place looked like every dungeon in every Hollywood movie ever.

"The last cell on the right," Leon said. "Your dad's in there too." He dropped back and let me go first.

Intrigued, I strode to the cell and stood at the

doorway. My father was on his knees, cradling my mother in his arms.

"Mom?" I said. My emotions went into free fall. For years, I'd believed this woman to be dead. My last childhood memory of her was in a car in Oregon when I was nine years old and she was telling me to run. I did as she asked and never saw her again until recently, when she'd been very much alive and in charge of a group of Cabal soldiers.

"Thomas," she said to my father, "I need to speak to him alone."

He nodded and said, "Of course" before getting to his feet and leaving the cell, laying a hand on my shoulder as he went.

"I don't have much time," my mother said, lifting her hands to show me a set of manacles adorned with magical symbols. "These things are draining my life away. The Cabal's idea of revenge for infiltrating their organization, I suppose. Before I go, I need to explain some things to you."

"You don't need to explain anything," I said. I didn't want her to feel she owed me anything, especially at this moment as she lay dying.

From somewhere deep within, I felt a stirring of the magic I'd recently discovered.

"Yes, I do, Alec. There are things you should know, such as the fact that I'm a member of the

ADAM J WRIGHT

Coven and I was never supposed to fall in love
with your father."

"The Coven?" I whispered.

She nodded weakly. "They are nine in number
now but there were ten of us when we formed
the Society of Shadows. When it became clear
that the human race was in great danger, I
volunteered to leave the Coven and infiltrate the
Cabal. First, I spent almost a decade working
with the Society while a false life and identity
was set up. It was during this time that I met and
fell in love with your father. When you came
along, I was torn between duty and love but in
the end, I had to perform my duty. Thomas
understood and plans were made to make it seem
as if he and I split up over a disagreement
regarding how you should be raised."

I remembered her taking me from England,
where my father worked, to Oregon where her
family lived. Or at least that was what I'd been led
to believe at the time. It was obviously all a lie.

"The incident in the car," I said. "The last time
I saw you. That was all a set-up?"

"Yes. We had to make it seem as if I was being
attacked by the Society. It was the only way I
could gain the Cabal's trust."

"And Dad knew you were alive all this time?"

She nodded. "Don't hate him for it. I told him
he had to keep my existence from you. It was part
of a larger plan. All of humanity was at risk.

Hundreds of years ago, I swore to protect the human race from its enemies. I upheld that oath, even though it cost me dearly."

The magic I'd felt a few moments ago became stronger. The black magic circle materialized in my mind's eye. As far as I could tell, this particular piece of my magic nullified spells. It had done so in Rekhmire's lair and it had stopped Merlin from casting a spell and sent him flying into Moosehead Lake.

My mother looked closely at me. "What's happening? I can feel magic in the air."

"These manacles," I said. "Are they using a spell to drain your life away?"

"Yes, there's a spell built into them. It's taken my power. I can't stop it."

"I can," I said. I concentrated on the manacles and allowed the black wave to emanate from me over the magical devices.

The white symbols on the steel dulled and the manacles split apart and fell to the floor.

My mother rubbed her neck and wrists. "You can tap into the Melandra Configuration. I didn't expect that."

Now I was confused. "The Melandra Configuration?"

She stood up and stretched, wincing. "When you were a child, the Coven asked your father to steal an artifact from the Society vault."

"The Melandra Codex," I said.

"Yes, the Codex. It had to be taken and put somewhere safe. The Society could no longer be trusted to have it in its possession because of the number of traitors in the organization. One day, the Codex will be used to save the human race; it was too risky to leave it in the Society's vault."

"So Dad took it."

She nodded. "And the nine witches who remained in the Coven performed a spell that would hide the Codex in a place it could never be found but could still be used when the time was right."

I knew what she was going to say next but I kept my mouth shut and waited.

"They wrote the contents of the Codex magically onto your bones."

"Yeah, I had an X-ray and discovered it."

"You've been tapping into its power," she said. "You cast a nullifying spell to take away the magic in the manacles. When the entire spell— which is called the Melandra Configuration—is cast, it is a million times more powerful than what just happened. The Configuration is known as the Spell to End All Spells. It nullifies all magic and seals the Earthly realm from all others."

"And it's written on my bones."

"A time will come when you'll need it, Alec. When that time arrives, you'll know what to do."

"I don't understand."

"You will." She gestured to the door. "Now, we need to go."

I wasn't going to argue with that. I followed her out into the hallway. Even though the manacles had been removed, she seemed to be in a lot of pain. When she saw my father, she collapsed into his arms.

He held her up and said, "We have to get her back to the Coven quickly."

"Back to the Coven?" I said, helping him guide her to the steps.

"Her work here is done," he said. "The enchantment that keeps her alive while she's away from the Coven's realm is fading. It only lasts as long as she's performing the task she came here to do and that's over now."

"But her life isn't," I insisted. "It can't be."

"Maybe if we get her back to her own realm, there's a chance she'll live," he said. Then he added, "Although there's no life or death in that realm so maybe live isn't the right word."

With Leon taking point in case we ran into any surviving Cabal members, we ascended the steps and left the castle. As we exited through the gate, I didn't look back. Excalibur was in the courtyard somewhere, lying among the bodies of those it had slain.

As far as I was concerned, it could stay there. I never wanted to see it again.

When we got to the bottom of the hill, Merlin

was conspicuous by his absence. I wished I could dismiss him as easily as the sword and hope I never saw him again but he was in Sheriff Cantrell's body and I was sure I was going to have to persuade him to leave.

"Gather around, everyone," my father said. "We're going to go to a place called Harbinger Academy and then we're going to get you all home." He looked at the two young girls as he said this.

"I don't have a home to go to," Cathy said.

Christina, who looked like her heart was about to break when she heard those words, knelt down next to Cathy and said, "Don't worry, we'll sort something out."

My father produced an egg-like item from his pocket. "We will indeed. But first, we need to get to the academy." He turned to my mom and me with a grave look on his face. "From there, we can get to the witches' realm."

He placed the egg on the ground and a portal opened that showed a number of large buildings clustered around a grassy area with a fountain.

Holding my mother tightly, feeling her strength fade away with each passing, I quickly stepped through.

27

"This is Harbinger Academy," my dad said as we went through the main door of the largest building. "We're going to train people. Much like the Society's Shadow Academy but better, of course."

"Dad, we don't need an explanation," I said. "Just get us to the witches."

"Yes, of course," he said. "Felicity, why don't you take the others to the kitchen and find them something to eat? I'm sure everyone must be hungry after their ordeal."

"I don't know where the kitchen is," she said.

"Just through that door and follow the corridor. You'll find it."

Felicity, Leon, Christina, and the girls disappeared through the door my father had indicated while he and I went to an elevator.

"Will this take us to the witches?" I asked, remembering the elevator in the Society HQ that had taken us to the Coven's realm.

"No, we have to go through my office," he said. "Don't worry, we'll be there in no time." He looked at my mother with a concerned look and gently stroked her hair.

"She told you about the Melandra Codex, I take it?"

"She did," I said.

"I knew the Society would eventually link me with its disappearance," he said. "I had to hide it somewhere where I knew it would be safe."

I looked at him with a hard expression. "On my bones?"

"Yes, on your bones. The spell contained in the Codex is very powerful. I had to leave it with someone I could trust; someone I knew would do the right thing when the time came. There's no one I trust more than you, son."

The elevator stopped and the door opened.

"Quickly," he said, leading me to a door that bore his name on a plaque.

We entered the room and he pulled aside one of the bookcases on the wall to reveal a green-lit passageway. He led me along the passageway to a set of stone steps that spiraled down to unseen depths.

"Shall I help you carry her down there?" he asked.

"No, I've got her. Just show me the way."

We descended as quickly as we could until we came to a room with an archway that was hung with a curtain of what looked like tiny bones. My dad pushed through it and I followed. I could feel my mother still breathing but her body had become limp in my arms.

The cavern of the witches was the same as I remembered. Huge and imposing with a raised rocky platform in the center. On that platform, nine cloaked figures huddled in a circle around a pool of black liquid.

As we approached the platform, my father spoke to the dark figures. "I've brought Sabina back to you. Her work on the Earthly plane is done."

"Then it is time for her life force to fade," said a female voice that rose from the pool.

"Her work is brought to its conclusion," said another.

"Like all mortals, she must die."

"Really?" I said, anger sparking inside me. "She sacrifices herself to do your work and you just toss her away when you're finished with her?"

"As you say, she sacrificed herself. She knew the price and she accepted it willingly."

"Well I don't accept it," I said. I'd had enough of being used as a pawn in someone else's game, of being controlled like a puppet by Merlin,

Excalibur, and now the witches. Enough was enough. I was determined to make the next move of my own free will.

"If you don't take her back, I won't cast the Melandra Configuration," I said. "I mean, that's what you want, right? For me to cast this ultra-powerful spell when the time comes? I won't do it. I'll never cast it, no matter the circumstances."

A hush descended over the cavern. My father fixed me with an icy glare and lowered his voice to an angry whisper. "Alec, don't threaten the witches. I've never heard of anything so foolish."

"You don't want mom to die, do you?" I shot back.

That made him turn his face away from me and become quiet.

"You will cast the Configuration," said a voice from the pool. "It is prophesied."

"Yeah, well prophecies are made to be broken."

The silence was deafening.

I waited. For some reason, they'd seen fit to give me their most valuable tool without my consent and now I was damned well going to use it for my own benefit.

"There is a way Sabina can rejoin our number," one of the witches finally said.

I stepped closer to the platform, my mother clutched in my arms. "Then do it."

"She may rejoin the Coven," said another voice.

"But," said another, "there will be a price."

28

"Price," I repeated. "What sort of price?"

"She will remember nothing of her time on the Earthly realm," said a voice from the pool.

"She will not remember ever leaving here."

"The entire journey will be wiped from her mind."

"So she'll forget me and my father," I said, pointing at my dad.

"She won't remember anything of the relationships she formed in your realm," said one the witches. The way they all spoke from the pool, each conveying the same sentiments in different ways, made them seem more like a collective than individuals. Would my mother become absorbed into the collective and lose every part of her personality that made her unique?

"There has to be another way," I said.

"There is no other way."

My mother stirred in my arms. "I'll do it, Alec. They're right, there's no other way. If I don't rejoin the Coven, I'll die. At least if I become a member again I'll be helping you, even if I don't remember that you're my son."

She looked over at my dad. "Thomas, I may forget everything that happened between us but please know that I don't regret a single moment."

The tears were in his eyes again as he nodded.

"Alec," she said, stroking my cheek, "I know you'll do what's right. I'm so proud of you." She smiled and kissed my cheek softly. "Now, I have to go before it's too late." I released my grip on her and she made her way to the platform while my father and I watched.

As she climbed the steps, two of the witches got to their feet and stood on either side of her while one of the dark figures on the far side of the pool also got up and waited.

My mother stepped into the pool and descended slowly into the black depths, as if walking down a set of steps. She kept going until the dark liquid swirled around her and she was completely submerged.

I heard my father weeping by my side. Then he gently whispered, "Goodbye, Sabina."

After a couple of seconds, she emerged from the pool, stepping up out of it, naked, toward the witch on the other side. A black robe was produced from somewhere and placed around her shoulders, the cowl arranged over her head.

The four standing witches took their places around the pool and sat, forming a circle of ten. They gazed into the pool and were it not for the fact that there were now ten instead of nine, the scene would be exactly as it had been when we'd entered the cavern.

A voice rose from the pool. "Leave us."

Turning away, my father and I faced the curtain of bone. He staggered slightly as if the strength had drained from his legs and I caught him, letting him lean on me as we made our way back to the curtain.

"I love her, Alec," he said. "I never thought it would end like this."

I guided him through the curtain and held him tightly while he wept.

"She may have forgotten us," I told him, "But we won't forget her."

29

An hour later, I stood on the roof of the academy building, leaning against the parapet and staring out across the endless sea of trees that stretched to the horizon. Everyone else was in the kitchen, eating and talking about their recent experiences. Talking things through was therapeutic but I needed time to reflect on what had happened at the Cabal castle before I spoke with anyone about it.

But that reflection could come later; right now, I just wanted to empty my mind and appreciate the beauty this realm had to offer. I could see why my father had chosen to build the academy here, even if the details of why he'd chosen to build an educational institution in the first place seemed a little sketchy.

When I asked him about it, he merely said that Harbinger Academy was a replacement for the Society's Shadow Academy but there seemed to be more to it than that.

I didn't press him on the matter. What he chose to do with his time was his business. Just as he'd said that he trusted me. I guessed that went both ways. Whatever he was doing here, it would be something that helped people, of that I was certain.

I heard movement on the roof behind me and turned to see Felicity walking toward me with a bottle of beer in each hand.

She handed one to me and said, "I thought you might like one of these. It's been a long day."

"It has," I said, raising the bottle to my lips.

"Wait," she said. "I propose a toast."

"All right. What should we drink to?"

"How about everything ending as it should?"

I thought about that. "Is that what you think happened here? That everything has ended as it should?"

"Apart from your mother," she said. "I'm sorry about that."

"It's okay. Although I'm a little worried about how my father's taking it."

"He's resilient," she said. "He'll be all right."

I nodded. "Yeah, I hope so. And he'll have you to watch out for him now that he's your new boss."

"Don't worry, I'll make sure he's okay."

"So," I said. "This academy. Do you think you'll be happy here?"

"I will. I think Harbinger Academy is going to do a lot of good and I want to be a part of that."

"Everyone in Dearmont misses you," I told her. Then I said what I'd actually meant to say. "I miss you."

"And I miss you," she said. "But there's no way I can come back now. The Society sees me as a way to get to your father. Things can't go back to how they were before."

"I know that," I said. I knew it but I didn't like it. I wanted Felicity back in Dearmont. I wanted to be close to her every day.

A silence descended between us. Felicity broke it by saying, "Cathy is going to stay here."

"At the academy?"

"She has nowhere else to go and we can help her learn how to use her powers. And when the other students arrive, there'll be lots of other people around, which will be good for her."

"What about Lydia?"

"She's going home but she promised to visit whenever she can. Cathy is glad about that. She's still feeling guilty about what happened."

"I'm sure she'll come to terms with it," I said.

"Yes," she said. "I'm sure she will. So now we can drink to everything ending as it should." She raised her bottle.

I clinked it with my own and we both drank.

"Speaking of visiting," Felicity said, "Maybe you'll visit the academy every now and then?" She looked at me with hope in her dark eyes.

I didn't need to be asked twice. "Of course."

"Good," she said, smiling.

The door that led to the stairs opened and Leon waved at us. "Hey, guys, everyone is wondering where you are. It's time to get Lydia home."

"It is," I said, pushing away from the parapet. "She must be desperate to see her mom again."

We went down to the first floor, where everyone was gathered by the front door. My father was watching over everyone like a mother hen. Lydia and Cathy were hugging and promising to see each other again soon.

My dad handed me one of the ornate eggs. "This will take you back to your cabin by the lake. Leon and I worked out the exact coordinates and I've put them into the device."

"Thanks," I said.

He threw his arms around me and hugged me tightly. "Take care of yourself, Alec."

"I will," I told him. "You too. And good luck with this place."

He smiled and nodded, wiping a tear from his cheek.

I went outside and stood on the graveled forecourt. Leon and Lydia joined me.

I looked over at Christina, who was standing in the doorway with the others.

"You coming?" I asked.

She shook her head. "I'm going to stay here for awhile. Your dad is doing some good things with this place and I'd like to help. It beats being spied on in New York."

"I get that," I said. I placed the egg on the ground and the air above it opened, showing the Pine Retreat cabin and Moosehead lake. With a wave to everyone standing in the doorway of Harbinger Academy, Leon, Lydia, and I stepped through the portal.

As the three of us set foot on the dirt road outside the Pine Retreat cabin, the shimmering portal closed behind us. The day was cold despite the sun being high in the sky. Since we'd been in Faerie, where time moved differently to everywhere else, I wasn't sure exactly what day it was.

Lydia shivered.

"I'll get a jacket for you from the cabin," I said.

She shook her head. "I'm not cold, I'm excited. I'm home. I didn't think I was going to make it. I thought I'd never see my mom again."

"Okay, let's get you back to her right now," Leon said. "Have you thought about what story you're going to tell her?"

She nodded. "I think I'll tell her I got lost in the woods."

He nodded. "She might go for that."

"I used to be a Girl Scout so she knows I could survive on my own in the woods if I had to." She looked from Leon to me. "I can't tell her the truth because she has very strong beliefs. If I told her about Faerie and magic and stuff, she might think I'm lying but she also might think I was taken by the Devil or something. It's just what she believes."

"Yeah," I said. "I met her. She isn't too keen on P.I.s."

Lydia shook her head. "No, she isn't. She thinks you're all in league with dark forces."

I winced at the suggestion.

"Maybe I should take Lydia home," Leon offered. "Otherwise, her mom might think you had something to do with her disappearance. She doesn't know who I am. I'll just say I was driving by and saw Lydia by the side of the road."

"When I finally found my way out of the woods," Lydia said.

"Sure," I said, seeing the sense in what Leon was saying. Mrs Cornell might be suspicious of Lydia's story and that suspicion might be increased if it was a P.I. who brought her daughter home.

"Thanks for saving me," Lydia said as she and Leon got into the Durango. I stood on the dirt road and watched them go until the vehicle was out of sight.

When I turned to face the cabin, I was

surprised to see Merlin standing on the porch. He stepped toward me. He held Excalibur in his hand. The sword wasn't covered anymore. Its blade glinted in the cold sunlight.

"Alec," he said, "you really have to stop leaving your sword behind. I told you before; she doesn't like to be abandoned.

"And I told you I was done. This is over." I pointed at Excalibur. "It's time for you to leave and give Sheriff Cantrell his body back."

He frowned at me. "You don't mean that, Alec. Look how well you and the sword worked together in that castle. Didn't it feel wonderful being able to vanquish your enemies like that? Just think what you could do together if you continued to work together. You protect people. It's what you do. Imagine how many people you could protect with such a powerful weapon by your side."

He held the sword out to me. "Take it. It's yours."

I took the sword. As soon as my hand closed around its grip, I felt energy surge along my arm. Before it could get any further than that, I whirled around to face the lake and hurled the sword as far as I could.

Excalibur spun in an arc, the blade flashing in the sun. As it descended toward the water, I felt relieved that I was never going to see the damned thing again.

Just as the sword was about to hit the water, a female hand and arm, clad in delicate chain mail, thrust through the surface and caught Excalibur's handle. For a moment, the sword and the hand were poised above the water, the sword's blade pointing straight up at the sky.

Then the hand descended, taking the sword with it into the depths.

I spun around to face Merlin. "The Lady of the Lake has taken the sword back. This is over. Now get the hell out of here and bring back the sheriff."

He offered me a thin-lipped smile. "I don't think I'll be leaving just yet, Alec."

I summoned up a rage that I knew would bring magic with it. I was willing to tap the deepest parts of the Melandra Configuration to blast Merlin back to wherever the hell he came from.

He stepped back and lifted his arms.

The next thing I knew, I was being hurled backward through the air. I hit the dirt with a force of impact that made the air in my lungs explode out of my mouth with a grunt of pain. I slid into the bushes by the side of the lake.

By the time I untangled myself from them and regained my feet, Merlin was gone.

He had Sheriff Cantrell's body and he wasn't willing to give it back. Meanwhile, the sheriff was trapped in some sort of ice prison on another realm.

Felicity's toast on the academy roof had been premature. Not everything had ended as it should.

Some things were still very wrong.

THE END

Don't miss the next book, Night Hunt!

Also coming soon...Skeleton Key: Harbinger Academy Book One!

Made in the USA
Middletown, DE
01 November 2019